LURKING FEAR

Violence and murder were far from the mind of Larcy Ryan, red-haired, blue-eyed and twenty-three, when she took the job of private nurse to David Magnam, a terminal cancer and heart patient in his late sixties.

Young Pete Crimmins did his best to persuade her to leave her post in that strange house on Lake Huron and marry him, but she wasn't quite ready for marriage . . . yet.

Of course David Magnam was a difficult patient; and of course he was afraid—of dying. Any man in his position would be. But that was not the only fear Larcy felt. There was menace and terror in every corner and cranny of that house—menace and terror that were inexplicable until she probed too deeply into its sinister secrets.

PUT PLEASURE IN YOUR READING
Larger type makes the difference
This EASY EYE Edition is set in large, clear type—at least 30 percent larger than usual. It is printed on scientifically tinted non-glare paper for better contrast and less eyestrain.

THE
BROODING
HOUSE

ALICE BRENNAN

PRESTIGE BOOKS • NEW YORK

THE BROODING HOUSE

PRESTIGE BOOKS INC. • 18 EAST 41ST STREET
NEW YORK, N.Y. 10017

Chapter One

LAKE HURON was no more than "a lick and a spit" (as her father would have said) from the house.

Larcy Ryan, crisp and fresh in the white uniform, her nurse's cap perched precisely on her short, red hair, smiled as she strolled down to the beach.

There was scarcely a ripple on the smooth, blue surface of the lake. Far out, a few fishing boats rode at anchor. An oar vessel moved slow and sedate, like a heavy woman, down lake towards port.

Later in the afternoon, a few hardy swimmers would brave the cold lake waters. It was middle June, but the lake water temperature hadn't as yet risen to a comfortable swimming level.

The sky was blue and serene, and the sun, as if apologizing for not making an appearance the day before, shone hot and bright. Three sea gulls flew overhead, uttering their eerie and lonely cry, as they dipped toward the lake.

It was a peaceful scene, like one of those picture post cards on which one writes "having lovely time, wish you were here."

Larcy breathed deeply of the tangy air before she turned, reluctantly, to go back to the house.

Two weeks ago she'd been overjoyed at the prospect of spending an entire summer so close to the lake.

"We have a motorboat of sorts," Mrs. Pierce had

told her, when she'd hired her. "So if you enjoy water skiing or fishing or boating, Larcy, the boat is yours."

Larcy had shaken her head. "I don't ski, and I don't fish, Mrs. Pierce. I guess the most I do is swim. But I'm very glad to be this close to the lake."

"I hope you'll be happy with us," Mrs. Pierce had smiled. The dark, thin brows had drawn slightly together. "My father is . . . rather hard to get along with. I have to be honest with you. He isn't going to make your job easy."

"He's ill," Larcy had said, calmly. "Most seriously ill people are hard to get along with, Mrs. Pierce. I'm not going to mind that part of it."

"He's dying," Mrs. Pierce had told her, biting at her under lip. "I don't know if you know or not."

"I know," Larcy had told her. "Dr. Ule told me all of the facts of the case."

"All of the . . . facts?" The woman's smoky eyes seemed to, suddenly, hold a wariness.

"That Mr. Magnam is a terminal cancer and heart patient," Larcy had said.

"Oh." The tension had seemed to leave her. "Yes, yes, of course."

Later she had said, in talking of Bena Pierce to her mother, "She's the most attractive woman . . . tall and slender, with a lot of thick, black hair with these bits of silver at both temples. She was very nice to me when we talked, but it was a kind of nice that shows on the surface. What I mean is that I don't think she gives of herself."

6

She amended that the next time she saw her mother. "She gives of herself to her husband. The way she looks when she even mentions his name . . . I never saw that kind of look on any woman's face before in my whole life."

Her mother, small and plump and pleasant-faced, observed that she'd thought Mrs. Pierce's husband wasn't living with her.

"Oh, no, I didn't mean it that way," Larcy had corrected her quickly. "What I meant was that he isn't living with her now. Because he's off somewhere with the navy. He's some kind of a big shot officer, I think. He writes her at least once a week, and you should see her face when she brings in one of his letters."

She had sighed wistfully and her mother had remarked, a bit caustically, that she was getting the wrong ideas about love. She was trying to make whole cloth out of romantic movie drivel. Love was warm and secure, like a candle glowing in the dark.

Larcy had flashed her a grin, and said that she'd put it very romantically.

However, Larcy had thought, with a touch of condescension, *her mother was pitifully out of touch. Love was fireworks exploding; bright sparks.*

She wasn't going to miss out on it, as she was sure her mother had. Oh, she and Larcy's father had seemed very happy with each other. But they had missed out on the fireworks. Larcy wasn't going to.

The path led up from the beach to a kind of open patio at the rear of the house. A rustic picnic table

7

and benches, and a fireplace, were set on flagstone placed haphazardly on the sand.

Bena Pierce sat on one of the benches, her dark head bent to a letter in her hand. She lifted her head and smiled vaguely as she heard Larcy approach. And then, immediately, went back to her reading.

There was a softness on her face, an inner glow, that was not lost on Larcy, and she thought wistfully, *I want to be in love like that.*

She had reached the back door when Bena's husky voice called to her. "Oh, dear, Larcy, I'm afraid I forgot. Father woke up very upset and insisted on seeing you immediately. Then the mail came—I completely forgot I was supposed to send you up to him."

Larcy felt her face flush. "I left him no more than fifteen minutes ago, Mrs. Pierce."

Bena Pierce looked sympathetic. "It wouldn't matter to father, if it was only three minutes ago, Larcy. Please try to put up with him, dear."

"Yes, of course," Larcy said. *I must remember that I'm a nurse,* she reminded herself. *And not a person who can afford to have nice, delicate ladylike feelings!*

David Magnam glared at her when she walked into the room. "Seems to me that when somebody's paid to work for someone, they ain't supposed to be gallivanting around doing what they want to do."

Larcy gave him a steady stare, and kept her voice carefully pleasant. "Is there something you wish me to do for you, Mr. Magnam? Are you in any pain?"

He said, his voice spiteful, "My dear Miss Bed-

8

pan—I prefer that, so long as I'm paying you, that you stay within hearing distance of my voice. If this is unthinkable to you, perhaps you'd be happier doing your nursing someplace else."

She saw him wait to see how she would take the "Miss Bedpan" bit. The first time he'd called her that, she'd left the room in tears, to her later chagrin. It had taken all of Bena Pierce's persuasion to convince her to stay.

After she had calmed a little, she apologized to Bena. "I'm ashamed of myself. I should have remembered that I'm a nurse. And that Mr. Magnam is ill and frightened, and he's taking out his fright on me because I'm the easiest and most accessible. I shouldn't have let it bother me. I'm sorry."

"Sorry?" Bena had said. "There's nothing to be sorry about. I'm just happy you're staying."

She moved to plump up David Magnam's pillows, and he slapped viciously at her hand. "Quit fluttering," he told her, his voice flatly contemptuous.

He stared up at her, the blue eyes spiteful, dulled and heavy by the months of pain. He was a caricature of a man, lying there propped up on the pillows.

Once grossly fat, with a protruding abdomen and sloping shoulders that seemed to be drawn over from the sheer weight of the pads of fat that covered him; he was now, in his illness, shedding the weight so rapidly that the flesh hung on him as if suddenly suspended from his bones.

"I don't believe you're really a nurse at all," he flung at her, his eyes suddenly suspicious. "You're much too young."

9

Larcy decided it would be best to humor him. She said cheerfully, "Did you mean that as a compliment, Mr. Magnam? I'm actually twenty-three years old and I've been out of nursing school for two years. But I don't mind you thinking I'm younger than I am. What woman would mind that?"

Larcy's youthful appearance had come close to losing her her first private nursing case. The husband had thought her much too young for the serious job of nursing his ill wife back to health.

Pete Crimmins, with whom she'd gone more or less steadily for the past year, had enjoyed it hugely. "Maybe I'd better back down on that offer of marriage I made you. I'd hate to have to go around correcting people that you weren't really my daughter, but my wife. It would make a guy feel pretty queer, don't you think?"

Pete! A half smile quirked at the corners of her mouth. She looked down at the man in the bed. "Would you like me to freshen you up a bit?"

His eyes narrowed and his thin lips seemed to thin even more. "She hired you, didn't she? That sweet daughter of mine? I figured she was getting tired of waiting for me to die. She hired you to do it for her, didn't she?"

Larcy said gently, "The only reason Mrs. Pierce hired me, Mr. Magnam, was because she thought a professional nurse could give you better care than she could give you. Her only concern was for you."

He gave a hollow, almost sobbing, laugh. "She's

got everybody fooled. What chance have I got against her? Lying in bed, helpless, while she goes around with that sweet look on her face, fooling everybody?"

He sent Larcy, finally, for a cup of tea from the kitchen. He made it an order, barking it spitefully at her.

In spite of her natural rebellion at being treated like a servant, Larcy felt a wave of pity for the man wash over her. To be so old, so sick, and so suspicious of everyone, even those closest and nearest. She thought what a horrible way it must be to live, and to die.

The mood of the house pushed against her as she walked along the uncarpeted hall toward the stairs. Gloom seemed to sift in through the opened windows like blown dust, and the sand that was almost a part of the furnishings.

When she'd first come, Bena Pierce had told her, "I don't know what you're used to, Larcy, but I don't attempt to keep the house in magazine cover cleanliness. Sybil (the maid-housekeeper) has all she can do to cook and do the light work. Dust doesn't bother me. I hope it doesn't bother you."

Larcy had laughed cheerfully. "My mother always says it isn't how much dust is in a house, but how much love."

Bena Pierce, she remembered now, had quickly turned her face away. Love, except perhaps, what Bena Pierce felt for her absent husband, was an unknown equation in this house, Larcy thought.

Sybil was in the kitchen, rather listlessly doing up

11

the breakfast dishes. She was a tall, gaunt woman with stringy brown hair which she kept plastered tightly to her head with hair pins and rubber bands.

She lifted her hands from the soapy water and darted a glance at Larcy. "You aim to do some cooking, you do up your own dishes. I got enough to do without having added work."

She had let it be known from the beginning that she wasn't fixing any "fancies" for Larcy, or for her patient, either.

If Larcy was being paid to take care of David Magnam, then she was being paid to clean up after him and herself, also.

Larcy kept her voice matter of fact. "I'm only going to make Mr. Magnam a cup of hot tea," she said. "I'll clean up whatever dishes I use, Sybil." She couldn't help adding, "I always do, don't I?"

The woman didn't answer. Instead she turned her back on Larcy, and made a great deal of noise rattling the silverware around in the sink as she washed dishes.

Larcy made the tea and carried it upstairs. When she opened the door and went into David Magnam's room, she found him asleep.

Or at least, pretending to be asleep. Larcy stared down at him for a moment, but he didn't open his eyes. At last she turned away and carried the tea back to the kitchen.

He hadn't wanted the tea at all. He'd only wanted to order her to do something; make her "know her place."

Larcy sighed. They weren't all angels during illness, like her first patient had been. But angel or not, each and every patient deserved her very best care.

She emptied out the tea and told Sybil that she'd wash the things she had gotten dirty, as soon as Sybil had finished at the sink.

The woman said ungraciously that as long as she was already doing dishes, she didn't mind a couple more, and for Larcy to leave them on the sink.

Larcy thanked her and walked out through the kitchen onto the patio. It was empty now.

She sat on one of the benches and gazed out across the lake. There was an island not too far out, a few trees jutted up from it. The sun was higher and brighter. Larcy had to fight the urge to go put on her bathing suit and take a quick dip. If she did that, Mr. Magnam, whom she didn't think was really sleeping, would surely decide he wanted her for something, and she would be caught in the wrong again.

She sighed unhappily. *I have no right feeling impatient*, she told herself. *He's ill. He's my patient.*

A sly, amused voice sounded at her elbow. She turned to face the mocking brown eyes of Lyn Francis, Bena's seventeen-year-old niece.

She was waggling a forefinger reprimandingly at Larcy. "Uh, huh, no nice nurse leaves her patient and goes for a swim."

As if she actually knew what I was thinking, Larcy thought. And stared at the girl's cold, insolent face.

"Lyn isn't really my niece," Bena Pierce had told Larcy, explaining Lyn. "She's a girl my sister Marian took to- raise. Marian loved children and never had any of her own. My sister spent quite a few

13

months in a mental institution. She died there. Does that shock you?"

Larcy had shaken her head. "Why should it?"

"I don't know," Bena had said. "It shocks some people. It's something I don't like to talk about."

"Of course, Mrs. Pierce," Larcy had said quickly.

She looked at Lyn now, lithe and pretty in a green-striped play suit, her legs smoothly brown, her shoulder length hair tied back off her face in a young girl style.

She swung to a seat on the bench beside Larcy. "Hi, Miss Bedpan," she said, her voice mocking. "That is one of the nicer names he calls you, isn't it?" Her lips twisted. "I wouldn't be a nurse for anything. Someone call me names and I'd conk them, sick or not sick."

She grinned at Larcy. "So it's very good for some people that I'm not a nurse, isn't it?"

"Oh, you'd get used to things," Larcy told her. "Sick people are rather like children. They get irritable."

The younger girl dismissed it by ignoring it. Instead, she asked, "How long do you think he'll hang on?"

Larcy stared at her. "What are you talking about?"

Lyn said, her voice coldly irritable, "Oh, come off it. You know very well that I'm talking about David. How long do you think it'll be before he dies?"

Larcy's shock must have shown in her face, she thought, because the girl laughed harshly. "Oh come now, don't tell me you don't know that him dying is the uppermost thought in Bena's mind? She needs his

14

money, and she isn't going to get it until dear David is dead."

She burst out laughing suddenly, "Oh, dear, I do wish you could see how you look!" She shook her head, "Someone really is going to have to tell you the facts of life. And the facts of life are these—if a person has money and someone else needs that money, then the thing to do is to try and get that money—on one way or another. That's Bena's predicament. She lacks the 'one way or another.' " She sighed, and her eyes flashed mockingly at Larcy, "And it's really too terrible, isn't it?"

Chapter Two

ON WEDNESDAY morning Larcy awakened, restless and heavy-hearted. She got up, dressed and walked over to the window. The rain streamed down the glass, glittering and oily. She could see the long shape of the boathouse, and beyond that, the lake, obscured now by the fog.

It's going to be a dismal day, Larcy thought, unhappily. Even as a little girl, rain had depressed her.

As she dressed, she found herself being fiercely glad that the next day would be Thursday and her afternoon off.

Her spirits lifted a trifle as she thought of the cheerful, bright atmosphere of her mother's kitchen. The smell of coffee . . . of cinnamon buns . . .

And Pete would certainly be there. He'd promised to come and get her tomorrow, so she wouldn't have to take the bus in.

There was a small glow of pleasure when she thought of Pete, tall and sandy haired and teasing.

She liked Pete. She liked him better than anyone she knew. If only he'd stop proposing to her every time they had a date!

Larcy frowned. She knew it would make her mother very happy if she married Pete. Pete was steady and good and reliable. In another year he'd be finished with college and then go to law school to become a full fledged lawyer.

There was an anxious feeling in her suddenly. She couldn't imagine Pete as a serious man making decisions; pleading someone's case. Who'd take him seriously? Half of the time he acted . . . and looked . . . like a fifteen-year-old.

She felt bleakly disloyal as she went downstairs. If your friends didn't have confidence in you, who would? But it wasn't, she told herself, as if she wasn't on Pete's side. She was on his side. It was just that . . .

She shrugged and gave up. Her rubber soles made no noise as she walked along the hall to the stairs. The house was silent, everyone presumably still asleep.

In the kitchen she raised the blinds and opened the screen door wide. The smell and sound of the rain penetrated the kitchen.

She made a pot of coffee. Her mother was fond of saying that there was nothing on a gloomy day for cheering a person up like a hot, strong cup of coffee. *So I'll try the recipe,* Larcy thought, grimly. Her conversation of the day before with Lyn had done nothing to make her job more bearable.

Even though she told herself that Lyn's whole purpose had been to shock, Larcy hadn't been able to throw off the feeling of dread that had taken hold of her.

It's too lonely out here for a young girl like Lyn, Larcy thought now. *There are no young people; nothing, really for her to do.*

In the two weeks Larcy had held the job, she had not once, she thought, seen one young person outside

17

of Lyn at the house. Nor had she ever seen Lyn in anyone's company other than Bena's.

She'd swim, or take out the boat, or lie on the sand sunning herself for hours. Or sit, cross legged on one of the benches on the patio, staring moodily out across the lake.

It's wrong, Larcy thought. *She should have young friends of her own age.*

As if on cue, Lyn appeared in the kitchen doorway. She was barefoot, and in blue-sprigged seersucker pajamas. With her hair rumpled about her face, she looked, at the moment, much younger than seventeen.

"I hope you made coffee enough for two," was her greeting. She flopped down on one of the kitchen chairs close to the table.

Larcy nodded. And got another cup and saucer from the overhead cupboard.

"I like rainy days," Lyn said. She propped her elbows on the table, and rested her chin in her hands. "Rain is gloomy and sad and lonely. And I like that."

She pulled the cup to her, after Larcy had filled it. "I suppose you like nice, bright, sunshiny days," she said. "Naturally, you would."

She stirred sugar into the coffee; tasted it. "You call this coffee? It's much too weak. Sybil makes delicious coffee. She isn't going to be pleased about you coming into her kitchen and taking over." She shook her head. "She's funny, Sybil is, but she and Bena get along fine."

She shrugged and sipped at the coffee. "At least

18

it's hot." And then, in an abrupt change of voice, "Tell me about your home. What's it like?"

Larcy stared at her across the table. "My home?" she said. "Why . . . why, it's just a home. Not elaborate or anything, and we need a new sofa . . . we've needed one for years, but mother always seems to use the money for something else. The kitchen always smells of something baking . . ." she shook her head. "It's just . . . home, I guess. Nothing else."

"What's your mother like?" Lyn said, insistently. "Is she like Bena?"

Larcy had to laugh. "Mom? She's nearly sixty and she looks like a mother. You know what I mean, gray hair, and too fat around the middle and . . ."

Lyn said carefully, "Bena doesn't look like a mother. No one would ever take her for a mother, would they?" She shrugged and grinned. "I suppose you've got a boy friend? A dozen boy friends?"

"Not a dozen." Larcy laughed again. "Pete's all I can manage at one time. He's a life guard. In the fall he goes to law school."

"Is he cute?" Lyn asked.

She's really interested, Larcy thought. *I don't know why, but she really wants to know these things about me.*

"Kind of," Larcy said. "He looks awfully young, though, and he's always teasing and . . ."

"Are you going to marry him?" Lyn seemed to be watching her face intently.

"I don't know," Larcy said. "I'm not in love with him, if that's what you're asking."

19

"Love?" Lyn gave a harsh laugh. "Don't tell me you believe in that old hat thing? Love. I'll bet some man made it up, so's it would give him a hold over some woman foolish enough to believe in the thing."

Her mouth thinned, and Larcy thought, *"She's thinking of Bena. I wonder why Bena being in love with her husband bothers Lyn so much?"*

Lyn got up and moved away from the table. "I hate smug people," she said, her eyes glaring at Larcy. "And you're very smug, aren't you? You think you've got everything, and you're a fool. Because you haven't got anything!"

After Lyn had gone, Larcy threw out the remaining coffee and washed the dishes she had used. Sybil hadn't yet appeared when she had finished.

She knew a childish feeling of satisfaction. "She won't even know I 'invaded' her kitchen," she thought.

When she went upstairs she found her patient still asleep. She went into her own room, picked up a magazine and tried to read. But she was too restless. Outside it still rained, a steady, monotonous, bone depressing sound.

Larcy gave up finally, and went back downstairs. She found Sybil in the kitchen. The woman turned and gave Larcy a look.

"I don't favor folks messing around in my kitchen when I ain't here," she informed Larcy.

Larcy gave a wry smile as she turned away. *I didn't win, after all,* she told herself.

When she went into the dining room, Bena Pierce, in a gray sheath trimmed in yellow, was coming

20

down the stairs. She looked as if she hadn't slept too well.

"Miserable day," she said to Larcy.

"Agreed," Larcy said.

"Father still asleep?" she asked. When Larcy nodded, she said, "Well, it's a good day for it. Have you had breakfast?"

"Only coffee," Larcy said, "which I made myself." She made a face.

Bena laughed. "Well, sit down and have breakfast with me," she invited. "Perhaps we can cheer each other up." She frowned. "I do wish it would stop raining soon. For some reason, the mail seems always to be late when it rains."

Larcy walked to the door and stared out. "I think I detect a smidgin of blue in the sky," she said. "Could be that it might clear up before noon."

Bena sighed. "And it could be that only your hope sees that blue, Larcy."

Sybil came in with a large platter of bacon and a plate of toast. When she was out of hearing, Bena said, sighing, "Sybil always cooks as if Johnson was here. I can't make her understand that we don't eat as much when he isn't here."

She took a piece of toast and broke it in half. "I prefer my toast unbuttered, but Sybil won't understand that either," she said wryly. She leaned towards Larcy. "I suppose you're looking forward to getting away from us for a few hours tomorrow?"

"I'll like seeing my mother," Larcy hedged.

"And boy friend?" Bena baited.

Larcy smiled at her. "Pete? I always like seeing

Pete. He's coming after me tomorrow. He has a car."
She grinned. "Of sorts."

"Bring him in, when he comes," Bena Pierce told
her, "I'd like to meet him. That is, if you wouldn't
mind."

"Mind?" Larcy said. "Of course not." Smiling a
little. "You'll like Pete. Everyone does."

When she looked in on her patient after lunch, she
saw that he was gripped with a pain that was threatening to overpower him.

Pity for him smote her. One thing she had to say
about him, he bore his pain well. The little pains he
overcame, and the big ones he fought until he was
exhausted before he gave in.

"Mr. Magnam," she said, "I'll get you something
for the pain."

She thought for a moment that he was going to
protest. He always put off having an injection as
long as he could. Because he was afraid?

Larcy tried to shake off the thought. She went to
the cabinet in which she kept her supplies, unlocked
the drawer and filled the syringe with a dosage of
morphine.

Bena had been puzzled at Larcy's insistence that
her supplies be kept locked. "Surely it isn't that you
don't trust us?"

"It's merely a precautionary practice," Larcy had
assured her. "We were taught in the hospital to be
extra careful of any drugs or medicines, and I can't
throw off the practice."

22

She deftly swabbed a spot on David Magnam's flabby arm and inserted the needle.

When she turned from the bed, she was startled to see Sybil's gaunt, bony form framed in the doorway.

It wasn't the first time Larcy had been aware of Sybil's watching eyes.

"Did you want something, Sybil?"

The woman shook her head. "No." And turned and walked away.

Larcy frowned as she sterilized the needle and put it back in its case before locking the drawer. Had David Magnam hired Sybil to watch her?

It seemed a preposterous thought. But David Magnam was a suspicious man. And had a right to be?

Larcy didn't want to think that one out. She waited until she was certain the medication had taken hold, and then she left the room, pulling the door closed behind her.

She was surprised to find Lyn outside in the hall. The girl seemed to have recovered from her anger earlier. She was dressed now, in shorts and a pink blouse.

"I thought maybe you'd like to water ski. It's going to be a beautiful day for it."

Larcy shook her head. "I've never been on a pair of skis. Even the very thought scares me."

Lyn stared at her. "And here I thought you were one of those people who aren't afraid of anything." She shrugged. "Could you handle the boat?"

"I'm not very good at that, either, but I could try." She gave a backward glance at the closed door be-

23

hind which David Magnam was sleeping a drugged sleep. "I couldn't leave until I was sure Mrs. Pierce would be here to watch out for Mr. Magnam. And then I couldn't stay away for more than an hour."

Lyn frowned. "Oh, banish the thought. I've already given up on the idea." Her lips seemed to tighten. "What's that stuff you give him when he has one of those pains of his?"

Larcy told her, and she said carefully, "It would be such an easy way to do it. An overdose. An accident. Who would question it?"

Larcy looked at her in horror, "How can you talk like that?"

Lyn gave a harsh laugh. "I suppose you've never had the thought that there were certain people who should be dead?"

Larcy said grimly, "I'm a nurse."

"You're a nurse!" Lyn's tone was mocking. "And that's supposed to give you completely angelic feelings? Nuts! I know quite a few people I'd like better off dead. You do too. If you'd be honest about it."

Larcy found herself shuddering as she walked away. Perhaps David Magnam's suspicions were more well founded than she'd thought.

Pete phoned early on Thursday morning that he wouldn't be able to pick her up. His car, he said, was in the garage. "Luck of the Irish," he complained sadly, "except I'm not Irish."

"I'll take the bus," Larcy told him.

"The tall, handsome gentleman waiting on the

corner, and wearing a white carnation, will be me," Pete said.

Larcy was smiling to herself as she hung up. On her way along the upstairs hall, as she passed David Magnam's room, she heard the harsh sounds of a quarrel going on behind the partly opened door.

Chapter Three

THE SOMBER house, awakening, stretching itself like an old woman with aching bones seemed to hold the sound of the voices, as if reluctant to loose them; then, as if tiring of the effort, let the voices roll, thunderous and loud and hating.

Larcy tried to pretend she was not hearing. She tapped her heels hard against the bare boards of the hall as she hurried to her room.

But the voices demanded to be heard. They rolled out from behind David Magnam's partially closed door, pounding and banging against Larcy's reluctant ears.

"Five hundred dollars," Bena's voice was thick and jerky. "You wouldn't even miss it."

"No!" David Magnam's voice wavered along the hallway, buried itself in the walls. "I warned you not to marry that man. He's been living off my coattails all of these years. Why else do you think he married you? I'll not see a dime of my money go to help him."

There was desperation in Bena's voice, hate. "Your penny pinching killed my mother," she said. "You wouldn't pay out the money for a decent doctor. I've never forgotten. Never forgiven." Her words sounded as if they were coming from behind tight lips, clenched teeth.

There was a note of subtle mocking in David Magnam's thin voice, "There's one way you can get the money," he told her. "You can . . . kill me. Maybe you can think of a way so that no one will suspect . . . maybe you've already thought of it."

"Maybe I have," Bena said, coldly and carefully. Footsteps sounded across the floor, the door was pushed closed.

The hall smelled of damp and mold and furniture oil, as Larcy, head bent, hurried along it. Bright sunlight, as if in apology for the rain and fog of the previous day, shone boldly in through the high, narrow window at the far end of the hall. Sybil was pushing a dust mop along the wide, uneven floor boards.

She glanced up at Larcy's approach and there was a look of hostility in the dark eyes. She said curtly, "It's not easy to live with someone as sick as he is. Even before he got sick he had mean ways. This here house . . . everything Mrs. Pierce has . . . is paid for out of his money." Her thin mouth twisted so that it looked thinner, longer. "He never lets her forget it. He don't think about her staying here, taking care of him."

Her dark eyes searched Larcy's face. She said, "Nurses aren't supposed to repeat what they heard, no more 'n a doctor or a priest. That right?"

Larcy said carefully, "I didn't hear anything, Sybil. My job is to take care of Mr. Magnam. That's what I was hired to do, what I try to do."

Sybil muttered something under her breath, as her tall, angular body bent again to pushing the dust mop. To Larcy it sounded as if she'd said, *Just you remember it.*

27

A flush stained Larcy's cheeks, and unhappiness darkened her blue eyes. She'd told Sybil she'd heard nothing. But she had heard. And the words crawled along her spine, shivered through her mind, words taut with hate and hating. She drew a steadying breath. Her job was to nurse, not to get involved. In fact, one of the first things a nurse was taught was that they were not to let themselves get involved in the personal lives of their patients.

She pushed a shaky hand through her red hair, and thought wryly that some things were much easier to say than to do.

She smelled the damp again, and the mold, and in spite of Sybil's dusting, there were grains of sand pushed up against the wainscoting and trapped there, glistening like diamonds when a ray of sunlight happened to touch them.

The bright sunlight pouring in, and the glistening sand and the normalcy of Sybil's dusting, seemed not to make a mark against the impenetrable gloom of the house. It was as if the rain still fell outside, and the fog smothered everything.

Larcy had felt it that first day she'd come, like a foreboding. Her steps quickened, and then she turned as a soft, mocking laugh sounded behind her.

Lyn stood there, leaning up against the wall beside the door of her room. Her eyes told Larcy she'd overheard the quarrel between Bena and David Magnam, and the exchange between Larcy and Sybil.

"Talking about dear Aunt Bena," she said, "she's nuts. Letting him run all over her. Letting Johnson

28

run all over her. I'd tell them both to go to hell if it was me."

Her brown eyes narrowed on Larcy's face. "I don't believe in a God," she said. "I never have. I don't think I ever will. But I say a prayer every night. Just in case. Know what I pray?" There was bitterness and hatred and scorn and hurt in her young voice.

Larcy shivered and a throb of longing hit her, a violent want to be home. Not later after the bus had gotten her there, but now. She wanted to be sitting in her mother's kitchen—her mother puttering at the stove as she usually was, the ties of her apron hardly reaching around her thick waist, the heavy sound of her feet as she'd walk from stove to sink to table.

She wanted Pete to be part of that scene, to be sitting across from her at that same table, his blue eyes boyish and brash, his lips pursed, whistling a tuneless ditty, the fingers of one hand tapping against the table in accompaniment.

There was a feeling of warmth in her as she pictured the scene, and it must have shone in her face, because Lyn said sharply, "What are you laughing at?"

Larcy shook her head. "I wasn't laughing," she said. "I was thinking . . . about my mother, my home, about . . . a friend of mine."

Lyn's eyes narrowed even more. She said coldly, "Your boy friend, of course. Why didn't you say it? Why do you have to be evasive about it?"

The slim, pretty face was ugly suddenly. She said, "About that prayer of mine, I pray that I'll never be fool enough to fall in love with any man."

The brown eyes opened wide, and she cocked her head to one side, like a bold, mocking bird. "Women like you and like Bena," she said, "make me sick to my stomach. Thinking you're so much just because some man makes you think he's in love with you. That's all it is, you know, pretense. If I wanted to let myself be made a fool of, I could have any manner of man tell me he's in love with me." She twisted around abruptly, and went inside her room. The door banged shut violently behind her.

Larcy stood still for a moment, staring. Lyn's movements had been so abrupt they had left her startled. She turned her head at the swish of the dust mop beside her, and looked into Sybil's dark, shadowed eyes.

Sybil said, "She's a bad one. Always was. Always will be. All filled with hate of Miss Bena, and after all she's done for her." The thin lips drew inward. "It's like she hates her because *he* loves her." The thick, unplucked brows frowned above the dark eyes. She said sharply, "Maybe it's Miss Lyn who shoulda been in that place instead of Miss Marian." She shook her head. "Some of the things she says, some of the things she does . . ." Her voice dropped off abruptly and she moved the dust mop on down the hall towards the head of the stairs.

Larcy, determined to escape before another scene could take place, found herself running the short distance along the hall to her own room. She went inside and softly closed and locked the door behind her.

There were two large windows that faced the lake.

This was what delighted Larcy about the room. She could close her eyes at night, and the sound of the water beating gently against the sand would lull her to sleep.

She crossed to one of the windows, drew back the criss cross white curtains that covered it, and stared out. The lake was very serene this morning, an azure blue, and pale green where the sand bars showed through. Two sail boats idled farther out, and in the channel, a heavy oar boat moved sluggishly down water towards the port.

The small motor boat that belonged to the cottage was drawn up onto the shore; three gulls perched on its helm. The cottage itself was set on a slight rise above the water.

Scrub pine grew to one side and behind and there was a flagstone patio, the stones set haphazardly into the sand, as if the labor had been hurried and without interest.

Bena had told her that Johnson, on one of his infrequent visits on shore, had done the patio. "He isn't," she'd said, with affectionate wryness, "a man who enjoys working with his hands. Physical labor bores him."

Larcy turned from the window and stepped out of her uniform and into a sweater and skirt. Her eyes were bright, clear and blue. Her red hair, free now of the stiff nurse's cap, was curled lightly around her cheeks, giving her the look of a clean, just dressed up, small girl.

She was in haste to get away from the somber, brooding house, with its aura of mystery and ugliness and violence buried just under the surface. She picked up her straw purse, checked to make certain she had her money, her lipstick, a compact, a comb, leaned forward to stare at her reflection once again, then left the room, closing the door quietly behind her.

The hall was empty now, as if the violence that had erupted so short a time ago, had never been. It was almost as if Larcy had imagined it.

She stopped before the door of David Magnam's room, opened it wider and stepped inside. He was lying flat as usual, his mouth partly open, his eyes closed. He was sleeping, or appeared to be.

Larcy tiptoed out again, leaving the door partly ajar, because of David Magnam's aversion to closed doors. She found Bena Pierce in the downstairs hall standing at the opened door, staring out. She turned as Larcy came down the stairs. Larcy thought she looked worn and haggard as if she hadn't slept the night before.

The smoky eyes grazed Larcy's face. She said, shaking her head, "You don't look calm and efficient, you look like a little girl going off to meet her first beau. Is he your first beau, Larcy?"

Larcy gave a small, embarrassed laugh. "Pete?" she said. "Oh, he's not that special. He's just . . . we just . . . like each other."

Bena said, "I thought he was going to come for you, that I was going to meet him."

Larcy made a face. She said, "His car broke down. It happens like that an awful lot. If Pete's supposed to pick me up, I never really depend on it." She shook her head. "It's an awful car, but it's all Pete can afford right now, and he's fiercely loyal to it. You should hear him talk about that car." She laughed helplessly.

Bena said softly, "He sounds nice." There was a wariness suddenly in her eyes. She said, "You heard my father and me." It wasn't a question.

Larcy nodded unhappily, and Bena Pierce sighed and said gently, "You're a nurse, Larcy, and you know how illness can disrupt a family. It brings tension and people say things they don't really mean. Such an illness as my father's when there's no hope at all, does terrible things to people's nerves. One is torn with pity and love and pain and helplessness."

Larcy found compassion in herself for the older woman. It *was* hard. A terminal illness was hard on everyone concerned. It twisted your nerves so that you said things you'd never otherwise say. Like . . . "You killed my mother. I've never forgotten. Forgiven." Like . . . "Don't think I haven't thought of it." A shiver rippled through her. She glanced at the slender watch on one tanned wrist. She'd given Mrs. Pierce the key to the medicine drawer earlier. She said now, "You understand about Mr. Magnam's medication? One quarter ounce every twelve hours? Oftener if the pain gets too bad. You know how to give it?"

Bena Pierce nodded. "Yes, Larcy," she said, her voice still gentle, "Dr. Ule instructed me in how to use the needle when it was necessary." Her voice dropped a note lower. She said, "I'm not trying to kill him, Larcy."

Larcy flushed. She said, "Mrs. Pierce, I shouldn't have been there in the hall."

Bena said softly, "But you were there, Larcy." There was a bitter sound to her voice. She asked, "Do you think I'm capable of doing harm to anyone, Larcy? He's an old man, he's in pain, he's dying. Do you think I'm devoid of pity?"

Larcy looked at the haggard face, the shadowed eyes, the pale mouth. She shook her head. "Mrs. Pierce," she said, "we all say things we don't mean. I've already forgotten what I heard."

A slight smile twisted Bena Pierce's well shaped mouth. She said, "My dear Larcy, if only that was true, if only we could forget so easily."

Her voice changed subtly. She said, "I'll drive you to the bus."

Larcy shook her head. "Thank you," she said, "but I'd rather walk. It's such a lovely day." She smiled at Mrs. Pierce hoping she wouldn't think it was *her* Larcy didn't want to be with.

Bena smiled in return and said, "I understand, Larcy. I like walking too. When walking one seems completely alone, and we all need these times of being completely alone. Have a nice day, and don't worry about father, I'll take good care of him, and I have your mother's telephone number in case anything should come up."

She turned away, the conversation ended. Larcy on her way to the door glanced into the living room that opened off the hall. Johnson Pierce's picture smiled mockingly down from above the stone fireplace.

Larcy stepped outside into the bright sunlight, the sparkling sand, the tangy smell of fish that never seemed to be completely absent. She climbed the slight rise that led to the highway. It was only a short distance along the highway to the bus stop, and it was a shady, pleasant walk, shaded by trees and mowed grass. Cars whizzed by, commuters mostly, she thought, who spent the summer at the beach, then drove like mad into town to their jobs.

She found herself thinking about Johnson Pierce. Which man was he? The one who could evoke something close to hatred in Lyn Francis? The one described in vicious tones by David Magnam as a man who lived on a woman's bounty? The one who could bring such tenderness to a woman's eye as even the mention of his name could bring to Bena Pierce's face?

Larcy sighed. The bus was coming, lumbering along. She started to run. Maybe he was all three.

Chapter Four

PETE WAS waiting when the bus pulled into the station. He looked cheerful, teasing, and wonderfully commonplace, in tan jeans and a flamboyant green and yellow sports shirt open at the throat.

He took hold of her by one elbow as she alighted from the bus. For a moment Larcy thought he was going to kiss her, right in front of all of the suddenly interested people, and she blushed.

"Hey!" Pete said, sounding delighted, "that red color goes real good with your red hair. What brought it on? Me?"

"Don't be silly," Larcy told him sternly. She turned to look up at him. "It's wonderful to see you, Pete," she said, and was so sincere about it that her voice quavered.

"Hey!" Pete said again. "Hey! I do believe the woman is finally getting around to appreciating me."

Larcy said, "Haven't I always?"

He let go of her elbow and caught her hand, swinging it as they walked. "Not that I noticed," he told her, in answer to her question. "Wish I could offer a cab," he told her, "but on my budget the best is the bus." He started her across the street to the yellow bus stop sign.

Larcy shook her head and drew back. "Who wants to ride on a day like this?" she asked him, "even in a cab?" Her fingers tightened around his. "Let's walk," she said.

"Anything to save money," Pete grinned at her. The sun was hot on the pavement. Here, there were no trees, only the sidewalk and the street with the moving cars, and the buildings one after another lining the street like marchers in a parade. A drug store on one corner, a bank, a jewelry store, a cafeteria, two five and ten cent stores side by side; a Coney Island, the spicy mustard smell steaming out onto the street through the opened door. In front of the big window facing the street were the steam tables with a tired, sweaty looking man forking shriveled frankfurters into hard looking buns.

Larcy turned her head and caught Pete's grinning glance. He said, "How's the appetite?"

"I think I can manage to wait until I get home," she told him, making a face.

"Hot dogs are very American," he chided her.

"So I've heard," she told him. "I still think I'll wait until I get home." They turned down a side street and after about a block the residential area began, the houses small and neatly painted with lawns out front and an occasional elm or maple tree casting shade up on the porches.

"How's Mom?" Larcy asked Pete.

"Bright as sunshine when I saw her this morning," Pete told her. "She was hurrying around baking a cake, and she had a roast in the oven. I think she worries that you're starving to death out there."

And then, as if it had been in his mind all of the time, he asked, "How long is your job going to last,

37

Larcy?" As if he was jealous of the job, as if it took too much of her.

A frown crossed Larcy's face. She didn't want to be reminded of her job; of the gloomy house on the beach; of Bena Pierce with her haggard face and her watching eyes; of Lyn; of David Magnam lying silently on his bed, suspicious, wary, hating. She gave a little shiver and shook her head. "I don't want to talk about it, Pete."

His blue eyes searched her face for a moment, and then he grinned. "Sure," he said. "I'd rather talk about a more important subject myself. Me."

She shook her head at him. "Pete!" she said. But there was a nagging anxiety in her. Maybe she should tell Pete the why of her reluctance to talk about her job. She knew her refusal to talk about it had been curt . . . She frowned, half turned towards Pete, and then wavered. What did she really have to tell, except for the quarrel between Bena Pierce and her father? And the very nicest of people said things in anger they didn't mean, hurled ugly accusations . . . She shook her head, decided she would not worry Pete with something she was not even sure was there.

She could see her mother's white frame house just ahead. She traced her lips with laughter and looked up at the tall, blond boy who walked beside her. "Race you," she told him, and started off at a high run.

Pete raced up the steps just behind her. "That wasn't fair," he told her. "Being a gentleman I had to let you win."

"Don't be silly," Larcy informed him, "you weren't being a gentleman at all. I always beat you." She gave him a smug grin. "That's because I'm much the faster runner."

The screen door opened before Larcy could open it, and her mother, pink and perspiring in a ruffled apron hiding a pale yellow dress put her arms around Larcy and kissed her and then stepped back and said, grinning, "She's breathing mighty fast. You have anything to do with that, Pete?"

"Sure," Pete said, looking resigned. "I let her beat me in a race."

Larcy said indignantly, "I beat him fair and square, Mom. I always beat him."

Her mother shook her head and Pete said plaintively, "Mrs. Ryan, can't you make her see it isn't ladylike to want to be the winner?"

Larcy's mother said slowly, looking at Larcy, "One of these days she'll learn it all by herself, Pete."

Larcy grinned at her. "Oh, I'm on to you," she told her mother. "What you're saying is that will be the time when I'll step out of childhood into maturity." She wagged a finger delightedly at her mother. "You're very obvious," she said, "and a little bit silly, but I adore you in spite of these faults."

"Listen to the girl!" Mrs. Ryan said, appealing to Pete. There was genuine affection in her face. "You'll stay to dinner," she told him. "There's all that roast of pork and that big cake, and with just two women to eat it, why it'd be a waste."

Pete grinned at her. "Well," he said, "seeing you put it that way."

39

Later, full of food, she and Pete sprawled on the grass in her mother's backyard and talked lazily of past days and of the coming fall when Pete would be returning to the university.

Larcy opened her eyes which she had closed, and looked up into Pete's boyish, handsome face. She said, and knew it for the truth, "I'm going to miss you. I'm going to miss you like anything."

"Come with me," Pete told her. "You can support me in style. A working woman for a wife. What guy wouldn't want that?" And then his young face became serious. "I'm not joking," he told her. "Except about the working part of it."

Larcy shook her head. "I can't, Pete," she said. "It's just . . ." she looked at him unhappily.

Pete said, gay and brash once more, "I'll say it for you," he told her, "you just don't love me."

Larcy glared at him and said stormily, "Pete Crimmins, can't you ever be serious about anything? Or anybody?"

Pete gave her his lazy grin. He said, "I've heard it takes one to know one." And then a frown rippled his smooth, tanned forehead. "Larcy," he said, "all jokes aside, something's bothering you. I've felt it since you stepped off the bus. Want to tell uncle about it?"

Larcy's eyes widened in surprise. "However do you know?" And then she shook her head. "Please, Pete," she said, "it's nothing to do with you. I just feel better not talking about it."

"Sure," he said, "sure. But if ever you feel that

you want to talk about it, no matter what, I'll want to listen. Okay?"

"Okay," Larcy said. Her voice was little more than a whisper. There for a moment Pete hadn't been the brash, bold boy she alternately lashed out at and adored, but a man, with a man's firm jaw and steady eyes that gave out security and confidence.

She pulled her eyes from Pete's, confused suddenly. She said, "It's just a feeling I have, Pete." She gave a little laugh, "and it's probably all imagination. My mother will tell you that I have the most vivid imagination."

She jumped suddenly to her feet. "Let's go over to the park and have a game of tennis," she said. "I don't have to be back until nine."

Pete stood up, long legged, lean. He said, frowning, "I ought to try and borrow a car, drive you back. I don't like to think of you having to ride that bus back, having to walk back there in the dark."

Larcy stared at him. She said, "Whatever has come into you? It's still practically daylight at nine o'clock, and everyone's outside, and it's only a lick and a spit, as my father would say, from the bus stop to the house."

"Just the same . . ." he said. He shrugged, "I'll go change clothes and get my racket. Pick you up here at the house."

Larcy nodded. She stood up, and her blue eyes searched his face. "Pete . . ." she said, a want in her suddenly to tell him about David Magnam . . . Bena . . . Lyn . . . Johnson Pierce who was not

41

there physically, but whose presence was always felt. About Sybil always sullen, always complaining, always . . . watching. About the ugliness, the violence, that seemed to pervade the very sills of the house.

Pete, his lean body half turned to leave, waited. Larcy wet her dry lips. And if she told Pete? What then? Wouldn't he tell her it was no place for her? That she should give notice she was leaving, tell Bena Pierce to find another nurse? And if she refused saying she'd taken the job and she had a duty to her patient, wouldn't he say that if she was so silly as to stay on in a house like that, with people like that, who might kill each other . . . or her . . . if the notion took hold of them . . . then her mother should be told and maybe she could reason with her?

A sigh built up inside her. In order to relieve herself of worries that might be unfounded, she was willing to worry Pete, worry her mother?

The sigh came out, soft, full blown. She forced a smile, shook her head so that her short red hair tossed against her cheeks and said, "Just . . . 'Pete' . . ."

"Just . . . 'Pete'?" he said. Lines of anxiety, Larcy noted unhappily, creased each side of his young face, and then he grinned and shrugged. "Sure," he said.

"I'll beat you at tennis," Larcy flung after him.

He turned and Larcy thought that his lightness was slightly forced. "Like fun," he told her. "That's one game I always win."

"There's always a first time," Larcy shot back, her voice carefully bright and impudent.

There's always a first time. What had she meant by that? Larcy asked herself fiercely. A first time to win a game? No, no, she hadn't meant that, had she? Then what? A first time for what? Murder?

The word dug itself out from her brain, posed vividly so that she could see each letter, feel it. She turned and hurried from the brightness of the backyard into the coolness of the house.

She was racing up the stairs to her room when her mother came blinking out of the kitchen. She stared up at Larcy, and wiped her hands on the ends of her apron. "What's all the noise?" she asked. "And where's Pete?" She frowned at Larcy. "You didn't have a quarrel with that boy, did you?"

"Now, mother," Larcy chided her mother lightly, "it seems to me that you have more affection for Pete than you do for me."

"Nonsense," her mother told her comfortably. "But I don't mind admitting I think he's the best son-in-law material I could get, and I'm not about to turn my head while a daughter of mine brushes off a fine prospect like Pete Crimmins."

A grin forced itself reluctantly across Larcy's mouth. She said, "I'm not brushing him off," and then, "and mothers aren't supposed to pick out their daughters' husbands. It's old fashioned."

Mrs. Ryan said, unperturbed, "It's an old fashioned idea then that ought to come back into use."

43

Larcy shook her head and said wryly, "I give up. I give up. But speaking about Pete, I'm supposed to be getting myself ready to go play tennis with him."

Her mother brushed a plump hand across her perspiring forehead, and said, "Tennis? On a hot day like this?"

"Hot days like this *are* for tennis," Larcy told her.

Her mother shook her head, muttered something under her breath about *crazy young people* and disappeared back into the kitchen.

Larcy went slowly up the rest of the stairs. Her room was cool, the blinds only partly drawn; the big maple tree out front, its leaves stirred by a vagrant breeze, cast shade into the room.

Larcy pulled the shades all of the way down to the window sill, found her white tennis shorts and a blouse in the closet, discarded her skirt and sweater and slipped into the shorts and blouse. She drew on white anklets and rubber soled shoes, tied her hair back with a yellow band, flicked a comb through her hair, studied her reflection with critical appraisal before going downstairs again.

She found her tennis racket and ball in the downstairs closet. Her mother glanced up as Larcy came into the kitchen. She gave her daughter an admiring look. "Don't get overheated now," she told her, "and don't spoil your appetite for supper."

"No, and no," Larcy told her, her lips curving in a smile. She dropped a brief kiss on top of her mother's hair.

"And don't win," Mrs. Ryan told her. "A young

lady should never plan on winning from a gentleman."

Larcy laughed as she pushed open the screen door on her way outside. She called over her shoulder, "I probably won't win, but that isn't saying I won't be trying." She shot her mother a gamin grin as she danced down the steps.

Pete lived only a block down the street. She watched him now as he walked along the back alley, swinging his racquet, his lips pursed as if he was whistling.

A feeling of dismay struck her. Only a short time ago he'd seemed adult, grown up, mature, and now he was a young boy in her eyes again.

Larcy looked down at her legs, long and slender and tanned beneath the white shorts. Two weeks at the beach had gotten her a fine tanning, at least. She smoothed the band around her hair. Pete was not a young boy, nor was he an adult man. He was Pete Crimmins, the boy she'd known for most of her life, the boy she'd gone steady with all through her high school years, the boy she'd probably end up in marrying, even though she might not be wholeheartedly in love with him.

She thought, unwillingly, of Bena Pierce, of the way her smoky eyes would search the clock, waiting for the moment when she could go to the highway and pick up the mail, of the way her face would change, like a young girl's face, as she'd read her husband's letters.

Larcy sighed and felt unaccountably cheated. She glanced up as Pete swung into the yard, and a slight blush stained her cheeks.

45

Pete's eyes were admiring. "Hey," he said, "you look like a kid. You look too young to be grown up, to be a nurse."

A coldness ran over Larcy as she thought of David Magnam telling her that, his eyes wary, pain filled, his voice twisted and ugly. He hadn't meant it as a compliment, Pete did.

Pete's eyes dug into hers. He shook her shoulders with mock ferocity. "Stop that," he told her.

Larcy's eyes lifted to his in bewilderment. "Stop what?"

"Stop going away when you're with me," he told her. "Stop thinking of someone else. I'm jealous."

She shook her head and gave a little laugh. "I'm not," she said, "and you're not."

"Two negatives," he told her, "ain't you been taught you should use at least one positive?"

In answer, Larcy swung around the side of the house and towards the front gate. Pete caught up with her and they walked slowly side by side, their hands not clasped, but touching ever so often as they walked.

Both courts were filled when they reached the park, and they wandered down to the artificial pond and watched the pair of white swans as they lowered their graceful necks to pick up bits of crumbs children and adults threw into the water.

Some of the watchers threw gum wrappers and cigarette packs and flipped cigar butts into the water. Larcy seethed and whispered in an aside to Pete, "Why do people have to do things like that?"

Pete shook his head. "Why do people do a lot of

46

things?" They turned away from the pond and walked back to the tennis courts. When one was empty they played two sets and Pete easily beat Larcy, who admitted readily that she hadn't been playing her best game.

Pete said, "Now, I suppose you're going to tell me you weren't trying to win."

"Oh, I was trying," Larcy told him, "but not very hard. You see it's psychological, I felt defeated before I started. I know you were going to beat me."

"Naturally," Pete smirked.

He left her at the house and Larcy showered, changed, had a leisurely nap, a cold sandwich and glass of milk with her mother before leaving to catch the bus.

Her mother eyed her anxiously. "You've not been yourself this blessed day," she told Larcy. "It's like something's troubling you." She waited.

Larcy sighed, wished her mother weren't quite so perceptive, and said, "They're queer people, mom, I'm not sure I understand them or . . . or approve of them."

The anxiety deepened behind her mother's eyes. She said, "If they're not nice people, then you shouldn't be staying out there."

Larcy said wryly, "Oh, mom . . . mom . . . I'm not a little girl." And then, "It's not that they aren't nice people, it's just . . ." she shrugged, gave up trying to explain, because if she couldn't explain things to herself, then she surely couldn't explain them to her mother. She carried her plate and glass over to the sink, rinsed them out. "Mom," she said,

47

"I'm a nurse. I don't have to approve of either my patient, or his family. All I have to do is to give him the very best care I'm capable of giving."

Her mother said, "As you always do." Her eyes stared down at the table top. She said, "This husband of this Mrs. Pierce . . . he doesn't stay at home?"

Larcy said, "He's in the navy, mom, I told you." Her eyes widened and she laughed as she saw her mother's face. She said, "Mom, it's not that, Mrs. Pierce is madly in love with her husband." She shook her head. "Stop thinking about it, stop worrying. If there was anything really wrong, I'd soon tell you about it."

She turned from the sink as Pete's blond head appeared outside the screen door. He came inside and Larcy hugged her mother, went into the other room to get her purse. "The bus leaves the station at 8:30 p.m.," she said. "I'll have to run." She hugged her mother warmly.

Pete looked at Mrs. Ryan, and said, as if to temper the sentimentality of the moment, "I suggested to mom that you'd feed me, but she said I wasn't married to Larcy," he flung Larcy a smug look, "yet, and until I was, it wouldn't hurt me to eat at home once in a while." He took hold of Larcy's arm. "We're going to have to run," he told her.

"Race you," she said.

He shook his head. "Oh no, you don't."

It was a nice night for walking, a soft breeze from the lake rustling the leaves, cars moving slowly now along the streets, the street lights just lit, children riding bicycles around corners.

The bus was just pulling in as they reached the station. They had a ten minute wait and they sat side by side on one of the wooden benches staring around the waiting room, watching the people who sauntered in, looking occasionally at each other, sometimes making small talk.

Pete said, "It's ready to leave." He got up and Larcy followed, hurrying past him to the bus. She handed her ticket to the driver and he punched it. Pete caught her hand. He said, "We sat here ten whole minutes and we spent most of that time not paying any attention to each other."

Larcy stared at him. She said, "But that's because we're so used to each other."

She had to board the bus. She stood for a moment on the bottom step, wavering. "Pete," she said frantically, feeling that she had to explain about today, "he's old and sick and he isn't going to get well."

Pete frowned. He said, "You've had other patients like that, Larcy. If it bothers you, then you shouldn't be a nurse."

She shook her head. She said, "I don't like him, Pete, and someone ought to like him, because you see, all of them hate him."

There. She'd said it. She'd told him. She had to move into the bus to make room for the others. She opened the window beside her seat and stuck her head out and waved to Pete.

She saw him still standing there staring as the bus moved out and past him.

Chapter Five

LARCY AWAKENED to movement in the hall outside her room. She lay taut and tense, unmoving. As a child she'd occasionally had nightmares. When she was overtired and overexcited, she'd hear sounds that weren't, see faces, scream in terror for her mother.

But she was no longer a child. She was sure that she'd been asleep, and an unfamiliar sound had awakened her. She opened her eyes, stared at the closed door, shadowy and unreal in the moonlight that filtered in through the half drawn blinds.

A wind had come up during the night and she could hear plainly the sound of the waves beating against the sand, and the whine of the wind. But these were familiar sounds she'd heard often in the two weeks she'd slept in this room. No, it had been something else. She flung back the light blanket that covered her, and walked barefoot to the door and listened. Nothing.

She carefully opened the door, but in spite of how careful she was, the door was old and warped and it creaked. She looked boldly out into the hall. If anyone was there, they could not possibly have failed to hear the creaking of the door.

Moonlight flowed in from the high window at the far end of the hall, touching only on emptiness. All of the doors were closed and silent, except David

Magnum's, and the yellow night light glowed dully behind the partly opened door.

Larcy stood for a moment listening, and then she went back inside her room, switched on the light beside her bed, found her slippers, stepped into them, pulled on a robe and went down the hall to David Magnam's room.

The somberness of the house pushed against her as she padded down the hall, and the sighing wind and beating waves had a dismal, forlorn sound. She shivered as she stepped inside her patient's room.

She moved towards the bed, and then stopped, her one foot seeming to be held suspended in mid air before she slowly let it down on the floor beside the other. Someone in this room was listening!

Her lips felt dry, her heart hammered much too fast. Listening for what? Nonsense. She forced herself to walk briskly over to her patient's bed. She turned on the light that was pinned to the wall on the left side of his bed, shaded so that the light would not shine into his eyes.

He was lying partly twisted to one side, his eyes closed, the thin waste of his face horribly emphasized by the shadows, his mouth partly opened, his light breathing raising his thin chest unrhythmically.

Her eyes searched the room, the corners, the screened windows, came to rest reluctantly on the closed door that led to the clothes closet. Unwillingly, and yet seeming to be impelled, Larcy went over, opened the door and looked inside, running her hand from one end to the other, as an extra precaution.

It was a very small closet, and anyone hiding inside it would be squeezed for space. Her breath caught and held for a second in her throat. Who did she think would be hiding in David Magnam's room? And for what?

She pushed a hand rather shakily through her hair and tried to laugh at herself. She'd overheard a quarrel between Bena and David Magnam and she was letting her imagination invent all sorts of weird happenings. Queer noises in the hall, people hiding in closets, yet! Shaking her head she went over to the bed to turn off the light. She'd stopped to see to David before going on to her own room when she'd returned from town.

She'd found him asleep and Bena had told her she'd given him a hypo just a half hour earlier. He had, she'd told Larcy, fought it but in the end he'd acceded and allowed her to give it to him.

"He's always afraid," Larcy told her.

Bena had frowned. And then she'd said, "Yes, yes, I suppose he knows, or at least guesses, he's going to die. Father's no fool." Her voice had sounded compassionate, full of pity. "Poor father," she said.

Larcy frowned now as her hand reached to turn off the light. People were actors, they could sound what they were not, say what they did not mean.

Her fingers found the button that switched off the light. She was moving away from the bed and out of the room when David Magnam's voice stopped her.

His voice was thick and slurred and his tongue seemed to have difficulty in forming the words. He said, "Thought I was asleep, didn't you?"

Larcy retraced her steps and stood looking down on him. She said quietly, "You should be asleep, Mr. Magnam." Her eyes sought the clock on the night table, with its illuminated dial. It said half past one.

He turned his head, and his eyes followed hers. He said, "You just getting back? A nurse who traipses around all night long while I lie here . . ."

Larcy didn't give him any answer. She waited, and presently he said, "What're you doing sneaking around my room, looking in closets, watching me breathe?" His voice wheezed and he closed his eyes for a second, opening them reluctantly and with difficulty. He flung his fear at her. "That stuff she give me," he said, "what'd you two do to it?" His wheezing became worse. "I wasn't supposed to wake up, that's it, ain't it?"

Larcy said gently, "Mr. Magnam, that's to quiet the pain and let you sleep. That's all it is. Dr. Ule prescribes it. He showed Mrs. Pierce how to give it to you when it's needed."

His lips looked dry and parched. He ran his tongue over them, waited a second and then spat at her. "You're all in cahoots together. You and Ule and Bena and that husband of hers." His voice came thin and weak and spent so that Larcy had to restrain the urge to put her hand over his lips, shut off the talking that was too much for him.

He gave a dry, cackling laugh, startling Larcy. "Philip had his eyes on my money, too," he said. "But Marian's dead and Philip ain't got a sneeze." His eyes opened slowly and he stared up into her

53

face. "What were you doing sneaking in my closet?" he shot at her.

Larcy shivered. It had been David Magnam she'd felt listening when she'd walked into the room, lying there in the dark, his eyes closed, listening, listening.

She drew a breath to steady her voice and said carefully, "I thought I heard a noise in the hall. I got up to see what it was."

He said, "You thought someone came in here? Hid in my closet?" His dry laugh cackled again. "I know what you were doing in here," he told her. "I know." His voice choked up for a minute and then came out, thin, vicious. He said, "I ain't going to die. You tell her that. I'm going to lay here and live forever. She ain't going to get my money for that husband of hers. Not one red cent of it."

Chapter Six

HE GAVE that dry, cackling laugh and closed his eyes. Larcy waited a moment and then said, "Good night. If you need me, ring. I always hear you."

She waited another minute to see if he would say anything, and when he didn't, she went out of the room, leaving the door partially opened.

She encountered Bena Pierce, clad in a white nightdress, her dark hair hanging in a thick braid over one shoulder. She was just coming out of her room.

Her smoky eyes searched Larcy's. She said, "I thought I heard father talking?" It was a question.

There was a coldness in Larcy. How could Bena Pierce have heard David Magnam talking? Unless she'd been in the hall. Unless she'd been near his room.

Larcy tried to stay the shiver that shook her. She said, "I thought I heard a noise in the hall, someone, something." Her eyes looked away from Bena. "I guess I was dreaming. I decided to go down and check on Mr. Magnam, seeing I was already awake. I'm sorry I awakened you."

Was there relief in Bena Pierce's face? She said softly, "You're a very conscientious person, Larcy. We're lucky to have you. Was father asleep when you left him?"

Larcy shook her head. There was a dry terror in

her. "He never wants me to stay with him. I told him that he was to ring if he wanted me."

Bena sighed and her voice sounded strained. She said, "When there's no hope, when there's only days and nights to be gotten through, so many, and then the end, it would be so much better if it could be over . . . sooner." She sighed again, the sigh seeming to rake through her tall, slender body, said "good night" to Larcy and went back into her room, her door closing softly behind her.

Larcy felt a chill as she walked the short distance to her own room. She went inside, closed the door behind her, and snapped the lock. She felt she was being silly, but there was the need in her to do so.

She took off her robe, folding it carefully over the foot of the bed so she could grab it quickly if the need arose. She stepped out of her slippers and placed them within easy reach.

She climbed into bed and lay there, her eyes open, staring into the moonlit darkness. Beyond the windows the waves still beat relentlessly at the shore, and the wind still whined.

She could count sheep. What was that silly commercial? . . . "I'm a nurse and I have to get a good night's sleep because . . ." She shook her head. It was no good. She wanted to erase Bena's words from her mind, and they would not be erased.

But she wasn't the first relative who had cried out against the mockery of living only in order to die in the end. People loved, they rebelled against pain for those they loved, they were filled with compassion and pity and helplessness.

And did she think Bena had meant her words differently? She rolled and tossed in the bed. There was something terrifying in the thought of David Magnum lying awake in the darkness, his eyes closed, but listening, watching, waiting, to die. Not by the disease that had laid its inexorable mark on him, but by the hand of someone.

She shivered again and pulled the blankets higher up around her throat. If she was going to keep on like this, then there was only one thing to do, tell Dr. Ule to find a nurse to replace her. Someone with less imagination, someone older, more hardened.

There was a reluctance in her to consider such a course. She felt almost a moral obligation to keep on a case once she had accepted it.

She turned her head towards the windows. The wind seemed to have lessened in intensity, and the waves held a soothing rhythm, lulling her to sleep, and that was what she wanted, wasn't it? To go back to sleep.

She'd heard nothing. There had been no noise. Only her dreaming. She yawned, stretched, breathed slowly in and out, in and out.

One of the large commercial trucks moving on the highway applied its air brakes and the sound penetrated Larcy's thoughts, but it was a familiar sound holding no terror for her, and the very familiarity of the sound calmed and reassured her.

Up on the highway, a young rabbit hopped across the road just in front of the truck, and one of the front wheels struck it, leaving only a ball of rubbed out fur on the sleek, glistening macadam. And a night hawk hunting, flew past Larcy's windows. It had been after the young rabbit, and was sore pressed to understand where it had hidden itself.

Lyn, in pink stretch slacks and a bare midriff top, was the first person Larcy saw next morning as, dressed in her uniform and soft soled shoes she was on her way into David Magnam's room.

Lyn's brown eyes looked angry and hidden, and her mouth twisted as she gave Larcy a scornful glance. "The angel of mercy," she said. "My, my, but don't we look pleased with ourselves."

Larcy held back the angry words that might have been said if things had been different and this wasn't her employer's house. Instead she managed to smile and say steadily, "Good morning, Lyn."

Lyn tossed her head fretfully and said, "It's not a good morning. It's a horrible morning." A frown ruffled her smooth forehead. She said, spite edging her words, "I could take him from you. Anytime I wanted to. I've always been able to do that. With anyone."

Larcy stared at her uncomprehendingly. "Take who away from me?"

"Him," she said. "The one you think you've got hooked. People like you are so silly, so terribly funny, so naive. I've taken lots of boy friends away from girls." She smoothed a hand down her slim front. "I don't want them afterwards," she said, and laughed. "But then neither do the other girls." Her face darkened. "It's what they deserve," she said. "Men!" she spat the word as if it was an ugliness inside her mouth.

Larcy was torn between the inclination to laugh and to be shocked. She said, "If you're talking about Pete, he's not *hooked* by me or by anyone. And you don't even know him." She stared bewilderedly at Lyn. "Why would you say that?" she asked her. "Why would you want to take Pete away from me, if he could be taken?"

Lyn shrugged. "Because it's exciting," she said, "and fun, and it makes other girls hate me." She laughed, and her brown eyes narrowed on Larcy's face. She said softly, "You're shocked. Admit it, Larcy, you're shocked."

Larcy said slowly, "Why do you want to shock people, Lyn?"

The other girl moved restlessly. "Don't lecture me," she said. "I hate it. Bena's always lecturing me, preaching. It's all mockery. I know Bena. I know all about her."

She traced a pattern on the hall floor with one sandaled foot. She jerked one hand at David Magnam's door. She asked, "He's still with us, I suppose. That's our kind of luck, isn't it?"

She laughed at Larcy's face and said, "There, I've shocked you again, and I didn't even try to." Still laughing, she went on down the hall.

Larcy stood for a second staring after her, and then went on into David Magnam's room. If she was going to let everything Lyn said upset her . . .

The utter absurdity of what Lyn had said made her want to laugh. Take Pete away from her. Pete! He should know. He'd be flattered. Or would he?

59

Suddenly Larcy frowned and there was a vague, fluttering uneasiness in her. What if someday a girl came along who would take Pete away. Not Lyn, certainly, but some girl somewhere. Pete whom Larcy didn't really want. Pete whom she didn't really love. How would she feel?

The uneasiness stayed with her as she raised the blinds, cranked David Magnam's bed up, smiled down at him, said "good morning." She pushed it aside. She was going to marry Pete someday probably, and they'd live happily forever afterwards.

The movie style love was for women like Bena Pierce, and she was no Bena Pierce. And face it, Bena, for all of her love for her husband, was certainly not the happiest woman Larcy had ever known.

David Magnam opened his eyes and stared up at her. Larcy was surprised at how well he looked. She said, "You look as if you slept very well. How do you feel this morning?"

"How do I always feel?" he growled at her. But surprisingly enough, he offered no resistance when Larcy washed him, readied him for his breakfast tray, gave him his first injection of the day.

"How about egg and tea for breakfast?" she asked him, carefully cheerful. She was prepared for his flat denial that he'd eat anything she brought him, but it didn't come. Instead he shrugged and said that he'd have to eat whatever she brought him, and who did she think she was kidding anyhow?

Larcy gave a polite laugh and went on downstairs to the kitchen. Sybil was busy at the stove and she did not turn around or let on in any way that she knew anyone had come into the kitchen.

"Good morning," Larcy said cheerfully, knowing her greeting wouldn't be returned. She prepared the egg and toast and tea and took the tray upstairs. As she reached the top of the stairs, the door downstairs slammed and, turning, she saw Lyn race out, clad in a bathing suit, a towel flung over one tanned shoulder.

She went on down the hall to David Magnam's room. He ate nearly half of his breakfast which was unusual. After she removed the tray, she cranked the bed down again as he requested, and brought him a pair of scissors and yesterday's newspaper.

He glanced up at her, his eyes heavy lidded and sly. He said, "You don't fancy my hobby, do you my dear Miss Bedpan?" His voice, scornful and mocking, raked down Larcy's spine.

One thin hand, trembling but triumphant, raised the newspaper so that she could see the front page. The headlines blazoned two violent deaths that had occurred the day before.

He lowered the paper and began cutting the items he wanted, those dealing with the two murders. Every so often he'd lift his eyes and look gleefully at Larcy.

He said, stopping his cutting for a minute, "Anybody who wants to murder somebody else can get away with it. All they'd have to do would be to find somebody with a motive and let them get stuck with it."

Larcy said nothing. She pulled the pillow from be-

61

neath his head, fluffed it, turned it over and put it back. David Magnam enjoyed baiting her. When she'd first come, he'd shown her his scrapbook, announcing gleefully that everything in it was fact, cut from newspapers. None of this fiction stuff, he said. All fact. Every murder, every suicide.

Larcy had stared at him, shocked, incredulous. He'd enjoyed it. She smoothed the blanket at the foot of the bed now, ignoring him, not allowing herself to be baited so that he could further enjoy his gruesome hobby.

She said, "If there's nothing more you want right now, I'll go downstairs and have my breakfast."

He was cutting again, and he didn't lift his head, or let on that he'd so much as heard her.

The hall looked cheerful and homey this morning, with the sun shining in the window, and a slight breeze blowing the curtains. Larcy, walking down the stairs could almost laugh at her fear of the night before. Almost.

She walked to the door and gazed out at the lake. Gray waves picked up gray-white sand and flung it on the beach.

The little breeze blowing in through the screen, lifted Larcy's hair back off her forehead. The front of the house faced the lake, with only steps leading away from the house and down the rise to the beach. In the back was the patio, facing the row of scrub pine.

As Larcy watched, she saw a man walking along the beach, quite a distance from the water. He stopped, shading his eyes with one hand and looked towards the house. He looked for a long time before he finally turned away and began walking again, stumbling along as if he was unused to walking in sand.

Larcy frowned, shrugged. There were always people walking along the beach. Why should she try and make something out of it? Resolutely she turned and walked into the dining room.

Bena Pierce, in a yellow shift, her dark hair piled on top of her head, turned slowly to face the doorway. There was a stiffness, a tenseness about her movements that seemed to disappear when she saw Larcy.

She smiled, pushed a hand along one side of her face and said, "Oh, Larcy, it's you." She waved at the table. "You couldn't have timed it better, Sybil's just made fresh coffee."

Her hand, brushing along her face, Larcy noted, was trembling. It was as if she had not expected it to be Larcy standing there in the doorway, and was pleasantly surprised when it was she.

"How is father?" she asked Larcy.

"He was clipping when I left him," Larcy told her.

Bena grimaced. "It's a gruesome hobby," she said, "but then if he enjoys it . . ." She shrugged. "A lot of people enjoy blood and thunder movies and books, the bloodier the better."

Sybil came in with the pot of coffee. Bena helped herself to a slice of toast. Over the coffee cup her smoky eyes met Larcy's. She asked, "Did you hear any more noises last night, Larcy?" Her eyes and her voice making light of it.

63

Larcy, pouring cream into her coffee, shook her head. "No," she said, "I must have dreamed it."

Beyond the dining room windows the sun shone on top of the picnic table, and the wind flattened the bits of grass striving for existence between the flagstones.

I did not dream it, Larcy thought. *I did not dream it.* Her hand, holding the knife, spreading jam on a piece of toast, shook.

Chapter Seven

LARCY WAS having a dream. A bad one. She shook herself awake, and stared vaguely around her. The sand was cool under her, and she glimpsed the lake through a veil of branches. She stretched her arms, yawned, the smell of pine sweetly, suffocatingly close.

She'd had a swim, lay on the sand in the sun, decided she'd had too much of it, and had gone up the slight rise into the shade of the scrub pine. She must have fallen asleep, she decided, alarmed.

She wondered how long she'd been gone. She thought unhappily, that she should have listened to Pete and bought herself one of those water repellent watches.

She'd left David Magnum still happily clipping from his newspapers. Bena had brought him two out of state newspapers someone had left on the beach.

Larcy had demurred against leaving the house but Bena had insisted. She'd put one arm lightly around Larcy's shoulders (an unusual gesture for Bena) and had told her lightly but firmly, that she hadn't been hired to spend twenty-four hours a day at David's bedside.

"You're young, Larcy," she'd said, her voice oddly wistful. "You need sunshine, fresh air, the water. Go on now. I'll see to father. He won't miss you. He never does when he's busily engaged in doing something he enjoys. An hour on the beach will do you worlds of good."

Had she been gone more than an hour? Larcy's fine brows drew together. Bena had seemed terribly insistent. As if she'd wanted Larcy out of the house?

Larcy pushed a hand against the sand, pushing herself to her feet. What a terrible way to think, and just because Bena Pierce had wanted to be nice to her.

She stooped over to brush sand from her knees, and then stayed in that position, bent over, uncomfortable.

The two figures were just below her, so that if she straightened, made any movement at all, their attention would become fixed on her. The sand felt rough on her fingers, and scratchy, and her muscles ached from the bent over position.

It was the voices that had stopped her, kept her from calling out to Bena Pierce as she and the stout, middle aged man stopped just below her, continuing a conversation already started.

The man's voice was thick and slurred. ". . . Sure he won't give you the money? Got to have it, y'know." His voice waxed impatient. "I told you. Warned you. Longer it goes, more money it's going to take. He ain't satisfied with the five hundred bucks. Chicken feed. Them's his words."

Bena Pierce's usually soft voice held panic. She said, "You didn't tell me someone else was with you. I thought . . ."

The man with her shook his head, said fiercely, "I told you about him. He's the one who thought it up

. . . got brains, y'know." There was admiration in his voice. "Never woulda thought of it myself."

Bena said bitterly, "It's blackmail. You understand that. Father knows. He said he'd never pay blackmail. Not to anyone." The bitterness slid heavier into her voice. "You know how he's always felt about Johnson, Phil."

The man's voice sounded angry, childishly angry. He said, "That don't matter to me. It ain't my concern. The money is. And if we don't get it . . ." He let his words drone away, like an airplane flying beyond sound. The threat was there, obvious, unhidden.

He moved one foot on the sand, pushing it around awkwardly, and Larcy, her eyes still, watching, knew a thread of recognition. The man she'd seen earlier far down on the beach, watching the house.

The man Bena Pierce had expected to see when she'd glanced up from the breakfast table and had seen Larcy standing in the doorway? The man she'd dreaded to see?

The man said carefully, "If he was dead you'd have the money."

Bena's voice sounded unhappy, pushed. She said, "How can you talk like that about someone? One would almost think you were suggesting . . . murder."

The man shrugged, said, "All in the way you look at it. If I was in his boots I'd want someone to do something about me; I'd ask them; invite them."

Bena said hollowly, "You're talking about my father, Phil, Marian's father."

"Marian's dead," the man told her. "He ain't nothing to me now. He never was. He hated my guts. All I want from him is the money. And if we don't get it . . ."

The two, to Larcy's intense relief, moved on down the beach towards the house, allowing her to straighten out of her awkward position, to move.

Larcy brushed automatically at the sand on her knees, her ankles, her arms, brushed it from her hair. Her mouth felt dry and scratchy as if she'd swallowed some of the sand. Her legs felt shaky, her knees seeming as if they might buckle under her. Bena must not know she had heard. It was a warning in her, a fear.

If she went down to the beach, Bena had only to look back over her shoulder and see her. And then Bena would know she'd heard.

The dryness in Larcy's throat got worse. There was only one way, to go back by the highway. She hadn't brought along a beach robe. She hung the towel she'd brought over her shoulders, hiding some of her bareness, then, shoulders back, eyes straight ahead, as if walking down the highway in her bathing suit was old hat to her, she started up the rest of the hill, skirting along the scrub pine until she reached the highway.

A red car filled with teen age boys whistled at her as the car came abreast. She kept a careful dignity, not letting on that she heard, that she saw.

Her heart was beating too fast, and perspiration ran down her back inside the towel, mingling with the sand, so that her back burned and stung.

She wondered what she'd say if she met Bena, how

she'd act. Would Bena know? She shivered and felt cold for a second. The gravel on the road that led down to the house cut into her feet.

It wasn't Bena she met, but Lyn who was standing just inside the hall door as if she'd been watching.

Her brown eyes widened when she saw Larcy and she said, mockingly, "What's in your mind, Larcy? To give the poor souls riding in cars a picture to carry with them? Why ever would you come down the highway in your bathing suit?" She shook her head at Larcy. "You look a sight."

Larcy, wanting only to shower and change, said, "I thought it would be quicker, and I was afraid I'd overstayed my time."

Lyn's thin brows arched. "Quicker by the highway? And all of that hot cement and gravel . . ." She shook her head, and her hair, hanging long and free, swung against the slender column of her throat. "You're lying," she said. "There's some reason." Her eyes stared mockingly into Larcy's. "Maybe you murdered someone," she said, "maybe you wanted to establish an alibi, make sure you were seen."

Her laughter bubbled forth at Larcy's look. She said, "You know, if I didn't know you were such a . . . chicken, I'd think you had gotten into something." She tossed her head impatiently. "Why do I bother with you? You're such a bore, Larcy."

Larcy let it go. She asked carefully, "Is Mrs. Pierce around? She was going to see to Mr. Magnam . . . she told me to go and she'd . . ."

Lyn cut off her words with an impatient exclamation. "I haven't seen dear aunt Bena," she said. "And don't ask me if I looked in on darling David, because I did not. He's not my problem, not even his money. You see, none of it is going to come to me."

Sybil stepped out of the kitchen, and said in her flat voice, "She told me to look after him. I just looked." She paused, as if struck by a thought, and said, irritably, "That's your job, not mine." She glared at Larcy, turned and went back into the kitchen.

Lyn laughed. "Bena's very attached to her," she said. She flung her hair out of her eyes and said slowly, thoughtfully, "Sybil'd do whatever Bena wanted done. Whatever."

Larcy said, "I'd better go change." Her eyes turned to look at the clock. An hour. She'd been gone no more than an hour. It had seemed longer.

She showered, slipped into her crisp white uniform, her soft soled shoes, brushed the sand out of her hair, perched the stiff white cap at just the right angle.

When she looked in on David Magnam he was lying awake, his newspapers piled around him, on the bed, sliding onto the floor. His scrapbook lay on the floor, half under the bedside stand, opened to the last page he'd been working on.

Larcy bent and began picking up the scattered papers. She said, straightening, a pile of them in her hands, "Have you had a good morning?"

He said irefully, "And if I have, it's no thanks to you, gallivanting off wherever you please, whenever you please, and on my time, my money."

Larcy piled the papers neatly on the table that

70

stood near one of the windows. She said calmly, "You don't have medication again until 8:30, Mr. Magnam, and it isn't lunch time yet."

He said, irritably, "That damn fool maid came up to ask how was I feeling." He mimicked Sybil's voice. "There's another one who does no more'n she has to do, and gets paid for doing it. My money." He sucked in his breath. "She's Bena's slave. She'd do anything for Bena. Always would. Sickening."

The hand Larcy smoothed down the side of her uniform shook. Lyn had said it too . . . *she'd do anything Bena wanted done. Anything.*

She finished piling the papers, put away the scrapbook. She looked for the scissors. When she couldn't find them, she asked David Magnam what he'd done with them.

His eyes looked at her fiercely from under the thick brows, the swollen, overhanging lids. "Why do you want to know?" he shot at her.

Larcy said quietly, "I want to put them away, Mr. Magnam, as I always do. In the drawer, so I'll know where to find them when you want them again."

"Never you mind about them," he told her. "I put them away myself. I want to know where they are, within reach. I might have a need for them one of these days. Protection."

Larcy knew there was no use in saying anything, he had this fixation . . . There was a sudden coldness in her. What if it wasn't a fixation? What if the things he dreaded were true?

The quarrel she'd overheard between him and Bena, the things Lyn let drop, the conversation she'd overheard on the beach between Bena and that man in which they had discussed his possible death and . . . blackmail.

A pinpoint of fear dotted the middle of Larcy's spine. Phil. Philip. One and the same. Magnam had called him Philip. He'd said, *Philip had his eye on my money, too. But Marian's dead and Philip hasn't a sneeze.*

She was aware David Magnam was looking at her, his eyes baleful. He said, "You don't like that, do you? You don't like me having them, do you? It scares you, don't it?"

Larcy said, "If you'd rather keep the scissors, I have no objection, Mr. Magnam." She saw he was perspiring. She said, "It's getting quite warm in here. Do you want me to turn on the fan?"

He didn't answer, and since no answer usually meant an answer in the affirmative, Larcy set the fan on the window sill where it would pull in the cool air from the lake, and plugged it in.

When she straightened, she stood at the window for a moment, staring out. The sky was blue, serene, the lake placid. She saw a lone figure walking along the beach, reach the slight rise, and she saw it was Bena Pierce.

She turned her head quickly, as if she felt Bena could see her, know she was standing at the window, watching. She knew she was being ridiculous.

David Magnam's voice had a fretful whine. He said, "I'm thirsty."

"I'll get you a pitcher of ice water," Larcy said. She picked up the pitcher from the bedside stand.

His voice stopped her. He asked, "Who were you watching out there just now?"

"Watching?" Larcy said. "I saw Mrs. Pierce coming up from the beach."

He said, "She went out with someone. A man. I heard them. She thinks I don't know what goes on. I know." He frowned and his eyes narrowed. He said, "I wouldn't be surprised if it wasn't Johnson who's put her up to killing me," he said, his voice vicious. "He thought he could put one over on me, marrying Bena. He thought he'd get it all, with Marian dead, you know. He thought I was going to die, but I fooled him, him and Bena both. I'll still be living after they're dead, the two of them."

Larcy said, "I'll get the water, Mr. Magnam." She saw that his face was contorted with pain after his outburst, but he made no outcry. He had courage. It was somehow pitiful to watch.

She was frowning as she went down the hall to the stairs. As she passed through the hall Johnson Pierce's picture seemed to smile down on her.

She stopped, turned her head to stare up at the pictured face. He was, she thought, one of the most attractive men she'd ever seen. It wasn't that he was handsome, because he was not. There was something about him . . . her frown deepened. The movies would call it a sex stimulus, the appeal of an older man.

She stared down at the water pitcher she held in her hands. Was he evil as David Magnam said he was? Had he really married Bena Pierce not for love, but for the money he hoped she would someday inherit from her father?

Her hand tightened around the handle of the pitcher. He didn't look evil . . . or perhaps he did, in a way, with those brooding, mocking eyes . . .

She turned sharply as she felt someone come up behind her, and met Bena Pierce's inquiring gaze.

Larcy felt herself flushing. She said awkwardly, "I was . . . admiring your husband's picture."

Bena's smoky eyes lifted to look at the picture. There was that softness again, sliding over her entire face. Larcy thought fiercely, *He can't be the way Mr. Magnam talks of him, and make her look like that. He has to be . . . good.*

Bena said, as if somehow she knew what Larcy was thinking, "Johnson's not good. Not in the way you think of good, Larcy. Does that shock you?"

Larcy said slowly, "Mrs. Pierce, I don't know how I think of 'good.' "

Bena said, as if Larcy had not spoken, "Father hates him. But he's always hated anyone I loved, including my mother." The softness was gone from her face, to be replaced by bitterness. And then, as suddenly, the bitterness left her face, and she smiled down on Larcy, as if Larcy was no more than a child. She said softly, "Wait for it, Larcy dear. Sometimes it takes a long time in coming. But wait for it."

Larcy swallowed hard and said nothing. She knew Bena Pierce was talking about love. The fire and the flame, the fierceness, the fireworks. Not the candle glowing softly in the darkness, as her mother said. She stared as if fascinated at Bena.

74

Bena said, "Oh, yes, Larcy, about that noise you heard last night. It must have been a rat. Sybil said she saw one in the kitchen yesterday morning. A large one." She gave a delicate shudder. "I've heard it said that if you see one rat you can count on there being at least one more you haven't seen. Sybil is going to set out poison. If she doesn't catch them soon, I don't know what to do. I can't call the exterminators with father ill in the house." The shudder again. "Don't tell father about the rat, he'd probably never sleep."

Larcy didn't have to pretend the shudder. It was there, rippling through every part of her body.

Bena said, sounding contrite, "I shouldn't have said anything. I'm sure Sybil will catch the horrible creature. She's very thorough at doing things."

Larcy repressed another shudder. It hadn't been a rat. Bena was making too much of it. Larcy had been willing to pass it off as a dream she'd had, but Bena wasn't willing to let it go at that. She'd had to search for an explanation. Why?

Because it had been Bena? Slipping down the hall to her father's room, looking for something in his room? A way to unlock the medicine drawer? Her mouth felt dry. What was it Lyn had said? . . . *It would be such an easy way to do it. An overdose. An accident. Who would question it?* . . . She couldn't repress the shudder that shook her.

"Oh, dear Larcy," Bena said. "I shouldn't have frightened you." Her tone changed subtly. She said, "Did you have a nice time on the beach, Larcy? I felt that I had to escape the house for a little while,

75

and Sybil said she'd see to father, and you're such a dear, conscientious girl, Larcy, that I knew you wouldn't be gone any more than the hour."

Larcy said, "I had a nice swim, and a sunning." She glanced down at the pitcher in her hand. "I'm supposed to be getting Mr. Magnam some ice water," she said.

Bena had lied twice. About the noise Larcy had heard, and about walking by herself on the beach. She'd needed to get Larcy away from the house . . . She'd known that Phil was coming. She'd gone off to meet him, hoping to stop him from coming to the house. Or . . . had she stopped him?

She filled the pitcher with ice cubes, ran water into it. She liked the coldness of the pitcher against her hands. Outside the kitchen window on the patio, a ground squirrel was pawing in the sand between the stones.

Larcy's heart gave a flop. Sybil could have seen a ground squirrel. At quick glance a person could think one a rat. Especially if that person was frightened, and afraid of rats. It didn't have to be a lie. Squirrels quite often got into the cottages.

She carried the water upstairs to David Magnam. She somehow couldn't picture Sybil as frightened. Not of a rat.

Chapter Eight

THERE WAS an uneasiness in Larcy. The fog was settling in earlier and heavier than the forecasts had said. Already it was shrouding the lake and the beach in a gray, impenetrable curtain.

The gloom of the house settled about her like the fog, moody, foreboding, cheerless. She closed the windows, pulled down the blinds, drew the curtains. The chill had penetrated inside the room.

She switched on a light, found a magazine, stretched out across the bed, idly ruffling through the pages. She'd left David Magnum asleep. Supper time was an hour away.

She read the first paragraph of a story, and then, bored with it, put the magazine aside, thinking wryly that if she were the author of the story, how depressed she'd feel.

She propped her elbows on the bed, resting her chin in her hands and stared thoughtfully at the headboard.

Bena hadn't reached David's room. *If* it had been Bena Larcy had heard, feeling her way stealthily along the hall. The creak of her door opening. Of course, that had been it. The noise Larcy had heard. Excitement laced with fear pounded in her.

If it had been Bena . . . she must keep remembering there was that *if* . . . why would she go to

David's room in the night like that? Why not in the daytime when Larcy was out of the house?

Larcy felt heavy, dull. It was too much, the noise last night, Bena and that man this morning, the fog. She rolled her body to the edge of the bed, slid her feet to the floor. She had to tell someone, talk to someone.

She fluffed a comb through her hair, smoothed the collar of her uniform as she stood up. Her mother? No, not her mother. She'd worry. Pete. Yes, yes, of course, Pete.

She had a sense of comfort as she thought of telling him. She thought of the way his blue eyes would look, crinkling at the corners with laughter, and then the lines smoothing out as she talked, and the laughter disappearing as he listened.

She could telephone him. There was always an hour after supper when she'd be on her own. She could tell Pete to drive out. She'd tell him to be very careful because of the fog.

She could put on her coat, they could walk along the beach. She could talk to him as they walked. The fog wasn't fearful when you were with someone you wanted to be with. It could even be comforting.

Her heart felt lighter. She switched off the light, plunging the room into a kind of grayish darkness. Curious how she'd thought of Pete . . . *when you were with someone you wanted to be with*. Her heart gave a tiny flutter. *Pete?*

Lyn was in the living room, sprawled on the floor, staring up at the mantel and Johnson Pierce's picture. She swung her head around when she heard Larcy come down the stairs. Her eyes were dark and mocking.

She said, "If I'd have been asked my choice, I'd have chosen to be born a man. I'd have made women bow to me, crawl."

Larcy frowned. She said, trying to make it sound light, "One would think you didn't like your own sex."

Lyn shrugged, staring down at her small, tanned hands with the pink tipped nails. She said, "Oh, I don't actually dislike my sex, it's just that most of them are so . . . spineless, so open to anything a man suggests."

She's talking about Johnson Pierce, Larcy thought. *Johnson and Bena.* As if impelled, her eyes shifted from Lyn's face to the pictured face that hung above the mantel.

Lyn's gaze followed Larcy's. Lyn said slowly, as if her words held an implication, "He knew Marian first, you know. It's how he met Bena.

"I lived with Marian. For a long, long time I thought she was my mother, and then I found out . . ." Suddenly, there was a lost look in the younger girl's eyes. She said fiercely, "She was good. Not like Bena. She shouldn't have had to die. It was all wrong. She had this . . . breakdown . . . she never was strong and Philip . . ." Her young face became set and hard . . . "He was brutal to her," she said. "He should have been the one, but it's never the way it should be, is it?" There was bitterness in her voice.

"She was going to come out of it, the doctor said, he had that hope, and then she had this operation and . . . she died. Bena was with her. Bena was always with her."

Coldness rushed over Larcy like the waves over the sandy shore when the lake was wild and stormy. What was Lyn trying to imply? That Bena had had something to do with Marian's dying?

Larcy knew it was ridiculous. The operation would have been performed in an operating room, even in a state hospital. There would have been competent doctors, nurses.

Lyn was hysterical. She was naturally bitter, first finding out Marian wasn't her mother, and then the breakdown and the death. But Bena could not be blamed for that.

But Lyn was blaming her. And Johnson? There was ice at the base of Larcy's spine. Why was Johnson Pierce being blackmailed by Marian Magnum's husband? Because he knew something neither Bena nor Johnson wanted known?

Lyn's voice came slyly. "Larcy," she said, "you look so terribly thoughtful. What are you thinking about?"

Larcy drew her thoughts back to the room, the fog rolling in outside the windows, Lyn staring mockingly up at her. "I was thinking," Larcy said slowly, carefully, "that I'd come downstairs to make a telephone call."

Lyn jumped lightly to her feet. "Talking about telephone calls," she said, "someone called when you were out. A man." Her brown eyes looked smug. "Pete, he said his name was. He sounded quite upset not to talk to you, but I made myself very charming to him. He said to tell you he had to drive into Ann Arbor, that he'd not be back by Thursday. I said I'd tell you."

Larcy stared at her unhappily. She'd wanted to talk to Pete. She'd thought of going to him with a real problem and he wasn't around to listen. She felt deserted.

Lyn said, "He sounds cuter than you said, Larcy. I'm going to have to meet him."

Larcy hardly heard her. There was a need in her, almost frantic. She could still phone Pete. Maybe he hadn't yet left, maybe if she asked him, he could put off going into Ann Arbor. She moved towards the telephone.

Lyn said nothing, turning her back on Larcy, as if completely disinterested.

But when Larcy tried the phone, it was dead. She felt such a letdown, such a sense of loss, that she nearly burst into tears.

Lyn said, "I could have told you the lines were down. They mostly are when it gets stormy." She gave a little laugh. "It's like a story right out of Hitchcock," she said, "the fog and the telephone lines down, and an old man dying upstairs."

Larcy shivered and Lyn laughed again. "One would almost think," she said, "that you expected something to happen."

Chapter Nine

ALL NIGHT she had disconnected dreams of roaming through the hall looking for something. She would try the door of each room, and it would seem to be locked until she put her weight against it, and then the door would push inwards throwing her forward. Bena Pierce would be there, just inside the door, her hair long and flowing around her shoulders like Lady Macbeth, and each time Larcy would push open a door Bena would say, looking sad and wistful, "Are you in love, Larcy?"

And behind Bena, her eyes flat and watching, would be Sybil. Larcy awakened again and again, in terror, only to fall asleep again and dream the same dream.

Outside, rain had replaced the fog. It was raining steadily, the gutters babbling like voices, the wind coming in through the windows and the walls of the house that wasn't too well put together.

By the time Larcy stopped dreaming, it was time to get up. The alarm went off, startling her. She reached over sleepily and shut it off, then lay for a moment, her eyes closed, every muscle in her body aching with weariness.

Reluctantly she slid her feet to the floor, stood up, found her houseslippers and robe.

By the time she was washed, dressed, readied for the day, she was agreeably surprised to find the fog lifted. The rain had stopped, the sun was shining. The only thing left over from the storm was the fresh, washed smell as she opened the windows.

When she walked out into the hall, closing the door of her room behind her, Lyn, dressed in green pedal pushers, her hair hanging long, and uncombed about her face, was heading for the bathroom.

She turned to look at Larcy, and yawned like a child, making no attempt to hide the yawn. She said, "The phone's still not working. I heard Bena trying it the first thing this morning. Before she was dressed, even. I looked out my door," she grinned mockingly at Larcy, " 'sneaked a look' is the right phrase, and saw Bena slipping downstairs and I went to the top of the stairs and watched her."

The brown eyes narrowed, searching Larcy's face. She said, "I wonder what dear aunt Bena has up her sleeve."

Larcy said carefully, "To see if the phone had been fixed, don't you think?"

Lyn said softly, "Who would she be calling? Aren't you even mildly curious, Larcy? Bena never phones anyone, unless it's the doctor or the grocer." She clicked her pink tongue against her teeth. "Johnson's out at sea, and his boat isn't due in port for a long time yet. And then, it's due at some foreign port. And Marian's dead . . . she doesn't have anyone to phone." Her eyes narrowed again and a half smile touched her young mouth. "Oh, yes," she said, softly, "There is someone. I'd forgotten, or almost forgotten." Her straw sandals lifted away from her heels as she clicked her way on down the hall.

The door of the bathroom slammed shut behind her.

Larcy looked fearfully behind her. As if she expected . . . what? She tried to laugh herself out of the mood Lyn had put her in, gave herself a mental shake and went on down the hall to David Magnam's room.

When she pushed open the door she saw Bena just turning away from the bed. Bena's dark hair was brushed neatly upwards and fastened on top of her head with two old fashioned tortoise shell combs, but she was still wearing her nightdress and robe.

She smiled when she saw Larcy, and said wryly, "I'm lazy this morning." She looked admiringly at Larcy. "So fresh and scrubbed looking, and even before breakfast. It's wonderful to be so young. I'd almost forgotten." Her smile deepened, but her eyes remained aloof and hidden.

She glanced down at David Magnam, who was lying flat, his eyes closed, the shadows under them deep purple, matching the veins that stood out so garishly in his hands that rested on top of the blanket covering him.

She said, "I dropped in to see how he was sleeping. I do that often. Sometimes he wakes up and just . . . lies there." Her voice dropped a notch lower. "Poor father," she said. Her eyes sought Larcy's. "Dr. Ule needs to be told," she continued, "that stuff he's giving him, it's not enough. It doesn't stop the pain. I can tell by his face . . ." She drew in her breath. "It's so horrible to watch, Larcy, to know there's nothing . . . you can do."

Larcy said nothing. Her eyes sought the clock.

Eight o'clock, almost one minute past. At home she was usually up much earlier. She glanced at Bena, said, "He's sleeping, Mrs. Pierce. He isn't in pain. He has his injection at 8:30. Most times he holds fairly well . . ."

"Just the same," Bena said, her voice sounding hollow and strained, "I'm going to phone Ule if they ever get that phone fixed . . ." Her voice waxed impatient. "The least little storm and the phone's out, the electricity's off." She moved restlessly, flung an apologetic glance at Larcy. "I'm sorry," she said. "I didn't sleep too well last night. The storm, and the wind blowing, and knowing the phone was out of order and that we couldn't get through to anyone if we had to . . ." She shook her head, sighed. "I kept thinking about that rat Sybil saw . . . I kept hearing it gnawing its way in through the walls." She shivered. "She set out poison . . . baited two traps with it, but she hasn't caught it yet, and until she does . . ." She shivered again.

She looked down at herself. "I'd better go get dressed, Sybil will have breakfast ready before I'm downstairs." She turned to leave, turned back to face Larcy. "Oh, yes," she said, "Sybil mixed it with peanut butter, the rat poison, you know. It isn't supposed to be fatal to creatures who can regurgitate, but then you never know, and I wouldn't want anything to happen . . ." she gave a weak laugh, "except to the rat, of course."

Larcy said slowly, "You needn't worry about me, Mrs. Pierce, I hate peanut butter."

The dark brows arched. "Well," she said, "I hope

the rat doesn't share your hatred of it." She laughed.
"I never touch it, not because I don't like it, but because it's so terribly fattening." Her eyes slid down
her slender figure. "Johnson," she told Larcy, "ab-
hors fat women. It's a phobia with him. He actually
gets nauseous."

The door creaked and Larcy turned her head to
see Lyn's green clad figure in the open doorway. She
said carefully, her brown eyes on Bena, "Marian was
fat. Mrs. 'five by five,' that was one of the prettier
names Philip used to call her." For a second the
young face was contorted by a mask of pure hatred.
Her eyes still held to Bena's face. She said softly,
"Marian never nauseated Johnson." She shrugged.
"Or at least he never let on in front of Marian. He
liked her . . . I used to hear them talking . . ." Her
brown eyes glazed over, she said carefully, "But it
was the money he liked, wasn't it, Bena? Not
Marian. And then you came along, and you were
prettier, more glamorous than Marian, and you also
were going to get the money, your share of it. So he
married you. And Marian's dead, isn't she? And
there's no one between you and the money . . . except . . ." The brown eyes looked downwards, at
David Magnam. "Except . . ." she repeated softly,
"David. And he's going to die."

Bena glanced at her in horror, and Larcy saw the
panic in her eyes. "You've no right . . ." she began unsteadily, shook her head, "such a thing to say,
to imply." She shook her head again, and her hands
flew to the ties that held her robe together at the
throat, tightening and untightening the knot. "You're

making too much out of a friendship. Marian was married . . . there was never anything. . . ." Her voice tightened, sharpened, "you were only a child, you twisted the wrong meaning into it . . ." her mouth wobbled at the corners. She said, "You don't understand, Lyn. Perhaps someday you'll understand . . ."

Lyn's voice was mocking. She said, "Oh, I understand, my dear aunt Bena. You're a fraud, a hypocrite, a liar. Philip at least let her know what he was, how he felt, but you and Johnson, you never did."

"Lyn, Lyn," Bena said, and there was sadness in her voice. She straightened her shoulders as if they ached. "I'd better go get dressed," she said.

Lyn watched her go, her eyes stormy. She looked past Larcy, to where David Magnam had not stirred. She said loudly, "He's a fraud, too, pretending to be asleep, when all of the time he's listening." She whirled around and raced to the door, letting it slam behind her.

Larcy walked over and opened it. Lyn was running down the hall toward the stairs. Sunlight slanted in from the hall window, making a halo above her head.

When Larcy turned back into the room, David Magnam's eyes were open and he'd turned his head so that he was facing her. He said, "She could stick a knife into a man without blinking an eye, but she'd do it from the front, not from behind."

One hand moved restlessly on top of the blanket. He said, "Bena's always tiptoeing in here, watching me, listening to me breathe." His dry, ugly laugh

87

cackled. "I fool her," he said. "She's never sure when I'm asleep, she's afraid I'd put up a struggle, raise all kinds of fuss. If she could ever be sure . . ." His heavy lidded eyes looked sullenly into Larcy's. "That stuff about Marian," he said, "she didn't have any guts. Bena's got some, but Marian . . . like her mother, weak kneed, whining, soft. That's what got her killed, softness."

Larcy found herself staring at him, protesting, "But Mrs. Pierce's sister died from an operation."

David Magnam gave what sounded almost like a chuckle. "Softness got her in that place in the first place," he said. "Got her heart broken, she did."

His face contorted and he said, "That stuff you give me, how soon before I get it?"

There was a wonderment in Larcy, a pity. It was the first time he'd asked for the injection. She looked at the clock, said briskly, "Another twelve minutes, Mr. Magnum. By the time I straighten your bed and freshen you up, it'll be time."

She exchanged the pillow behind his head for a fresh one, took the slip off the pillow and put the pillow aside to be taken downstairs, aired and fluffed. She sponged his face and hands, smoothed his bed, and by the time she had the syringe filled, it was eight-thirty.

His eyes closed as she slid the needle under his skin. She withdrew it skillfully, swabbed it off with alcohol, replaced it in the drawer, locked it, and put the key carefully in the pocket of her uniform.

She wasn't aware David Magnum was watching her until she walked over to the bed. He asked slowly,

"You carry that key everyplace with you?" And when she nodded, he said, "Somebody'd have to break the drawer open to get inside it, wouldn't they?" His eyes held hers. "Unless," he said, "they had another key made, and that wouldn't be hard to do."

Larcy said, "I'll go bring you some breakfast now."

He said, his voice impatient, "Don't want any breakfast."

Larcy said coaxingly, "I'll bring you up a tray. You might change your mind when you smell food."

He didn't answer her. The hall was bright with sunlight, but as she walked down the wide stairs, the eerie cry of a gull, lost and lonely and forlorn, sent sparkles of coldness up and down her spine.

Bena was sitting at the dining room table, sipping at a cup of coffee. She looked up and smiled at Larcy who had to pass through the dining room on her way to the kitchen. "I'm just having coffee," she said, "I'm waiting to have breakfast with you, Larcy dear."

Larcy said, "Your father hasn't eaten yet, Mrs. Pierce. Sometimes it takes him a long time to eat a little . . . perhaps you hadn't better wait for me."

There was a wistful sound to Bena's voice. She said, "It's lonely always eating by yourself, Larcy, the food has no taste. Lyn hasn't eaten yet, but one never knows about Lyn. There are times when I'm not sure if she ever eats breakfast."

There was movement in the doorway, and Lyn whirled in, seating herself in the chair across from Bena, making a very loud noise about it.

"Dear, dear aunt Bena," she said, "you can stop

89

your worrying about me. That's what you were doing, isn't it? Worrying. I'm here. I'm going to eat breakfast. I'm going to keep you company, so that you won't die from loneliness."

Larcy saw Bena flush, but her lips curved in a smile as she glanced across the table at Lyn. Sybil came in carrying a pot of coffee, which she set on an asbestos mat in the center of the table.

Lyn poured herself a cup of coffee and grinned mockingly at Bena. "You do look so happy to have my company, auntie dear," she said.

In the kitchen Larcy fixed a tray for David Magnam, toast, an egg, tea, orange juice, marmalade. As she passed through the dining room carrying the tray, Bena had her head down, seeming to be concentrating on her cup of coffee. Lyn, both hands curved around her cup, was staring deliberately at Bena's bowed head, as if by the act she could force Bena to lift her head, look at her.

Outside the door of David Magnam's room, Larcy removed the sauce dish containing the marmalade. The bitter taste of the orange peel would make it easy to hide a slightly more bitter taste, wouldn't it?

But Sybil had mixed the poison with peanut butter for the rat. Wasn't that what Bena had said? Peanut butter? Larcy partially repressed the shiver that shook her, but she did not return the saucer of marmalade to the tray.

After David had finished the little he wanted, Larcy carried the tray out into the hall. She stooped down to pick up the saucer she'd left beside the door. It was gone.

She stared unbelievingly. It had to be there. She remembered setting it down outside the door.

She heard a noise, something that sounded like a scraping sound. The rat Bena said Sybil had seen? The one she'd baited a trap for with poisonous peanut butter?

She waited, listening, muscles tense and aching. But the sound was not repeated. The hall was empty, quiet, sun filled. Forcing herself to a steadiness she did not really feel, she went downstairs.

Sybil glanced around, her eyes sullen, as Larcy came into the kitchen. She said, "I picked up that saucer of jam you set outside his door."

Larcy stared at her. She said, "It was a silly place to set a dish, but I would have brought it down when I brought the rest of his things down."

Lyn's voice sounded high and shrill from the other room. "Oh, for heaven's sake, Larcy, who were you expecting to eat jam from a dish off the floor? Sybil's rat?"

Larcy felt pressured, pushed. There was also that small ball of fear in her that kept rolling around, turning over and over. She set down the tray and walked into the dining room. There was a slight rise to her usual low pitched voice as she said carefully, "I admit it was a crazy place to set the dish, but Mr. Magnam didn't want it . . ." It was only a little lie, she told herself, and perfectly permissible under the circumstances. She didn't allow herself to dwell on what 'under the circumstances' entailed.

Larcy found herself watching Bena Pierce. Bena's eyes were wary (*and frightened?* Larcy wondered), behind the mask of wry sympathy. "Father," she said, "makes all sorts of weird requests. He could have asked Larcy to throw the whole miserable mess out of the window, and been very upset if she didn't honor his request." She shook her head at Larcy. "Sit down and have some breakfast, dear Larcy," she said, "and don't pay any attention to either of them. You and I know father and his moods."

Larcy gave a wan smile and sat down. She hadn't said it had been David Magnam who had wanted the saucer of marmalade set out in the hall. Bena had said it. All she'd done was not to say anything.

Lyn gave her hair a fretful toss. "Such a to do about nothing," she said. She watched impatiently as Bena poured coffee from the pot into Larcy's cup. "There's nothing to do around this place," she said. "There's no excitement." The brown eyes stared across the table at Bena. She said softly, "A murder would add some excitement, spice things up around here." Her eyes narrowed and she sounded as if she was reading something. "The victim," she said, "mistakenly used peanut butter in which arsenic had mixed . . ." Her eyes moved on Bena's face. "Oh, my," she said, softly, "it wasn't arsenic, was it, auntie dear?"

"It wasn't arsenic," Bena said calmly.

Sybil, as if she had been listening, came out of the kitchen carrying a plate of muffins. She said, her flat, dull eyes looking at Bena, "I caught that rat," she said. "And I burned it and the rest of the poison in the fireplace. Ashes are still smoking in here."

A chipmunk perched on the sill of the window was

seemingly oblivious to the humans inside, the floating sound of distant laughter sounded, and a chill crept its way up Larcy's back.

Lyn said, her voice soft and mocking, "Now there's no need to worry, is there? About the rat, of course."

Bena appeared to ignore her. "Drink your coffee, dear," she told Larcy, "before it gets cold."

Far, far down on the beach, on a cutoff that led down from the highway, two men sat in an old model car, stared away from each other, and argued in fierce, low tones that got out of hand every once in a while, to be cut off, hushed, started again.

One of the men was short, dumpy, middle aged, with dull, hating eyes and a bloated face that was crisscrossed with fine, blue veins. The other man was thinner, younger, with hungry eyes, a cruel mouth, and a bright purple striped jacket.

The sun was bright and hot. Children poured out of the houses bordering the beach, a young girl, curved and tanned in a bright blue bikini spread herself on a blanket on the beach in front of the car.

Neither man so much as looked.

Chapter Ten

ASHES STILL smoldered in the stone fireplace on the patio. Larcy had not been able to keep herself from looking.

She poked a stick in the powdery ashes. There was no smell of burned flesh, and wouldn't there have been if Sybil had burned the rat as she'd said?

She threw the stick in the fireplace, and when she turned around, Sybil was there. She gave a quick glance at the fireplace, and then her eyes, partly hooded by her lowered lids, turned on Larcy, and she said, "The phone's fixed, if you want to use it now. She told me to tell you."

"Thank you," Larcy said politely. It was queer how Sybil seemed always to speak of Bena Pierce as "she," not "Miss Bena," not "Mrs. Pierce," but "she."

Sybil flung another look at the fireplace. She said, "It's a good morning for burning. Wind's just right to stir up the flame, take away the smell."

She walked back across the patio to the kitchen, her oxfords making little more noise than Larcy's soft soled nurse's oxfords.

Who had told Bena she'd tried to use the phone last night? Lyn? But of course Lyn. Who else was there?

Larcy walked quickly down the little rise of sandy hill that led to the beach. It was not a morning to dwell on anything depressing. It was a gay, beautiful, sunshiny day, a day in which to be happy.

The beach was deserted at this hour of the morning. Only the gulls were there, spreading their wings, stretching out a leg as if seized by a sudden cramp. And two jack snipes walking with their curious stiff legged gait along the edges of the water.

Why would Sybil burn the poison if she'd caught only the one rat? Wasn't it Bena Pierce who had heard if you saw one rat there was at least one more you hadn't seen? Why wouldn't Sybil bait other traps? At least see if there *was* more than the one rat?

She moved along the beach, and the jack snipes moved along just ahead of her. A lone gull whirled to a stop on the water far down the beach.

She thought of Pete . . . she could phone him . . . She shook her head as she walked, and a feeling of unhappiness stirred in her. Pete would already be gone. Hadn't Lyn said he was going to Ann Arbor, that he'd still be gone on Thursday?

She stooped down and picked up a handful of sand and let it sift through her fingers. She thought of David Magnam saying that Marian had had her heart broken. By whom? Her husband? Bena? Johnson Pierce? ·

Johnson Pierce who had wanted only David Magnam's money and had seen Bena Pierce as a more sure way to it than Marian?

A shiver ran through Larcy and she turned quickly around and headed back for the house. The sun wasn't really warm, and the wind was sharp and the sand felt cold as it sifted through her fingers.

Dr. Ule came in the afternoon. He was a tall thin man with salt and pepper hair that barely covered his scalp, and a protruding stomach in spite of his thinness.

He seemed very sympathetic towards Bena who managed to look wan and lovely and pale as if she bore the whole burden of her father's care alone.

He took her by both shoulders and shook her gently. "Stop it now," he told her, "we're doing all that can be done for your father. It isn't going to help him any for you to break down."

He looked at Larcy, his pale blue eyes washing over her face. "I'm increasing the morphine," he told her. "Every eight hours." He patted Bena Pierce's shaking shoulder. "He isn't in too much pain," he told her. He shook his head in evident admiration. "For a man of his age and his condition, he's holding up longer than I would have thought possible."

Larcy saw Bena Pierce's head jerk up. She asked, her voice soft, choked, "What will happen when the . . . . morphine won't touch the pain?"

The doctor's eyes slid from Larcy's to Bena's. He said carefully, "When it becomes necessary he'll have to go into the hospital." He stared past her into the other room.

Bena said fiercely, "It's so terribly, terribly unfair. Everything."

Bena walked out to the car with him. She walked like a queen, Larcy thought, almost with envy. When she turned around Lyn had come up and was standing behind her.

There was mockery on Lyn's young face, making it look older, harder. She said, "Bena hoped Ule would give her hope. He didn't offer her any real hope, though, did he?"

Larcy said, "She's concerned about him."

Lyn laughed. "Concerned is the word all right. Bena's really concerned . . . about how long it's going to be before she can count on having his money. I think Johnson's trying to push it. He's quite a gambler. He's probably gotten himself into a jam with the wrong people. It wouldn't be the first time." She grinned at Larcy, "Some of those guys play pretty rough, you know."

Larcy thought, *It could be that . . . his gambling.* Bena had called it "blackmail," but she could have meant it was blackmail to have to pay a gambling debt when gambling was illegal. It could be that. It didn't have to have anything to do with Marian Pierce's death.

And then Lyn, whose moods Larcy had found were strange and unpredictable, whirled around and fled up the stairs, saying, "This house is much too gloomy. I'm going to get dressed and go into town."

There was the soft purr of the doctor's car taking off, and the hall door closed behind Bena. Her face looked strained. She smoothed one hand along the side of one cheek and said, with a soft little sigh, "I think I'll go get into my bathing suit and have a swim and a sun bath."

Larcy said, "The wind's still chilly. You'll freeze."

Bena shook her head and smiled, a set, tight smile. "I'm tough, Larcy, much tougher than I look."

For some strange reason, her words sent a chill through Larcy.

The afternoon was long and dull. Bena had spent most of the morning at the beach. When she picked up the mail and found no letter from her husband, her face set in lines of despair, she had only coffee and a bunch of purple grapes for lunch.

Afterwards she went up to her room. Lyn had not returned from town at lunch time. Bena seemed not to notice. Sybil griped and complained in the kitchen that she'd fixed lunch, spent her time, used up her energy, and nobody had hardly eaten a bite.

Larcy moped about the house, finding it even more lonely and disagreeable in the empty silence. At least Lyn slammed, shouted, raced, made noise.

At two o'clock Bena came out of her room in search of aspirins. "Hasn't Lyn come back yet?" she asked, and when Larcy said she didn't think so, Bena sighed and said, "She drives too fast, it's an old car and the tires are thin. One of these days . . ." She sighed again, looked sad, and went down the hall to the bathroom.

The wind had turned hot and dry. It blew into the house, bringing the gritty taste of sand with it. Shouts of swimmers sounded, far off, laughter, horns blowing up on the highway.

In his room, David Magnam alternately dozed and growled. He insisted Larcy bring him the day's newspapers, his glue and his scrapbook.

He pulled his scissors out triumphantly from under his mattress, shooting Larcy a smug look to see if she was watching. He soon tired of his clipping and irritably told Larcy to take the stuff off his bed.

Larcy put the heavy book on the table by the window. In doing so, she let the book fall and when she picked it up, a clipping fell out. Unlike the other clippings, it had not been pasted into the book. The date of the newspaper had been rubbed out, and the name and the town.

The headlines were large and black, blazoned across the whole front of the paper . . . *Man Accused of Killing His Wife Acquitted.*

Larcy hurriedly stuffed the clipping back inside the scrapbook, but not before she had caught the name of the accused man. Ronald J. Pierce.

Her hands felt icy. J. for Johnson? She turned from the window to find David Magnam watching her, his eyes wary and probing. "What did you find just now?"

She shook her head, did not look at him. "A piece of paper," she said, forcing her voice to calmness. "I put it back in the book, Mr. Magnam."

He seemed satisfied, but you could never be sure about David. She smoothed his bed, fluffed his pillow, got him fresh ice water from the kitchen. When she came back, he was sleeping, his mouth slightly open, his breathing loud and regular.

She went into her own room, closed the door behind her, took off her uniform, flung herself lengthwise on the bed and tried to read.

Tiring of the effort, her eyes seeming to be heavy and weighed down by the heat that poured into the room, she flung the book aside, went down to the bathroom, had a shower, changed into a fresh uniform, looked in again on David, and went downstairs.

The kitchen was empty, the house gloomy in spite of the sunlight that flowed in, empty and unbearably silent. Larcy wandered outside, stood at the kitchen door gazing out at the two garbage pails and the wire trash container.

A movement near one of the garbage cans caught her eye. She turned her head in time to see a large gray rat slink its way past the garbage cans, the trash container, passing almost directly in front of her.

She gave a squeal of pure terror, unable to control herself, and dashed back inside the house, to lean weakly up against the wall beside the kitchen door.

Sybil *had* seen a rat. It hadn't been a lie! She felt almost tearful with relief. She opened her eyes and looked up when Sybil's voice sounded dully from the doorway that led into the dining room.

"You sick or something?" The dark eyes with their heavy lids were turned relentlessly on Larcy's face.

Larcy gave a weak laugh and shook her head. She said, "I saw a rat. By the garbage cans. It ran right in front of me. It was silly of me to scream . . ." She passed a hand shakily down the front of her face, as if brushing aside what she had seen.

Sybil said, "Most people are scared of rats." Her eyes probed Larcy's face. "I caught a rat," she said, "this morning in the trap."

Larcy said firmly, "There's another one. I saw it, just now. A large one." She shuddered.

100

Bena came into the room, a silk robe flung over her slip. She was shoeless. Her smoky eyes stared at Larcy, "What happened?"

Larcy felt embarrassed. Before she could answer, Sybil said, "She saw a rat. Out by the garbage cans, scared her, I guess."

Bena looked from Sybil to Larcy and back again to Sybil. She said softly, "The poor child, I don't blame her for being frightened. I was afraid there was more than the one . . . you'll have to catch it, Sybil."

The woman nodded. "I'll catch it," she said. "I'll put the traps out tonight."

Larcy almost said, "But you don't have the poison, you burned it." She kept herself from saying it. Sybil, as if she'd read Larcy's mind, said "You don't need poison for a trap. All that's needed is to set it in the right place."

"Of course," Bena said, smiling sweetly at her. She turned to look at Larcy, said, "Poor Sybil, she's frightened to death of poison, never likes to have it around." She shook her head gently at Sybil, looked back at Larcy. "Johnson used to keep a revolver in the house when he'd be home." She shivered, laughed softly, "He kept it under his pillow, and I never made his side of the bed. I couldn't bear to lift the pillow, pull up the sheet, for fear the gun would go off."

She shook her head again, laughing at her fear. "At first he thought it was a joke, but he doesn't keep the gun around anymore, at least not under his pillow."

Sybil began taking things out of the cupboard beside the sink, making a great deal of noise about

101

it. Bena watched her for a second, then said, in a soft, amused voice to Larcy, "I do believe Sybil is letting us know that we're in her way." She tucked an arm through Larcy's and walked her out into the hall.

Larcy glanced down at Bena's stockinged feet. She said, "I'm sorry I made such an idiot of myself, screaming like that, as if I'd never seen a rat before."

Bena said, "I was going to get dressed and come down anyway, Larcy, dear. I was trying to read, but the room's much too warm, and I half believe I got a slight sunburn this morning. At least my back feels as if I did."

She drew her arm out of Larcy's and then halfway toward the stairs, she turned and looked full at Larcy. She asked softly, "What did you find in father's scrapbook, Larcy?"

Larcy stared at her, frowning, not understanding at first. Her face cleared when she realized Bena Pierce was talking about the clipping that had fallen out when she'd dropped David Magnum's scrapbook. Ice formed hard and tight around her heart, and little fingers of fear chased up and down and around inside her.

"Oh," she said, "you mean the clipping. It dropped out of Mr. Magnam's scrapbook as I was putting it on the table."

Bena Pierce pointed out gently, "Larcy dear, father always pastes his clippings after he cuts them out. Always."

Larcy shook her head. She said firmly, "This one wasn't pasted in the book, Mrs. Pierce." She said logically, "If it had been, then it would not have fallen out."

"But of course you're right." Bena appeared to give it some thought. "I wonder . . ." she said . . . She frowned . . . "Larcy, dear, did you notice the date of the clipping?"

Larcy shook her head. "No," she said. "There was no date on it."

"The name of the newspaper?" Bena persisted gently.

Larcy's throat felt dry and tight. She said, "I only glanced at the clipping, Mrs. Pierce, as I was picking it up, but I'm sure, almost sure," she corrected herself, because she hadn't read all of it, "that the name of the newspaper wasn't on the clipping."

"Oh?" Bena's brows arched questioningly. She frowned, shook her head, grimaced. "I suppose," she said, "father clipped it out and then decided it wasn't bloodthirsty enough for him. He likes his murders violent and horrifying." She appeared to be waiting for Larcy to say something.

Larcy said slowly, "I wouldn't know, Mrs. Pierce. I didn't read the clipping. The headlines were something about a man acquitted of killing his wife. I wouldn't know the details."

"Oh," Bena gave a quick, tight laugh. "That explains it. He wouldn't be interested in the details of the trial after it was over. He probably has the clipping about the murder already pasted in his book." She grimaced again. "If he was doing research to write a book or something . . ." She shook her head.

"It's a gruesome business, the way he's so fascinated by the most horrible of crimes." She put one stockinged foot on the bottom step. "I think I'd better go get dressed."

Larcy watched her ascend the stairs, and then turned and walked out to the patio. She leaned against the redwood table, gazing up at the scrub pine that rose twisted and dwarfed, on the sand hill above the house.

How had Bena known he'd dropped the scrapbook? That something had fallen out of it?

How had she known unless she'd been watching from the hall outside David Magnam's room? Watching for what? And why was she so interested in the clipping?

Because it concerned Johnson Pierce? Because Ronald J. Pierce was in reality Ronald Johnson Pierce? Her husband?

It looked dark in the scrub pine, dark and shadowy and haunted. There seemed something evil and ugly about the twisted trunks, the branches that leaned crookedly into the wind, as if the struggle for survival had left the trees weary and defeated.

Larcy fled down to the beach, pursued by fearful thoughts, haunted by the house and its inhabitants.

Chapter Eleven

THE NIGHT, silent and oppressive, lay like a great, dark shadow over the house. Larcy lay in her bed staring up at the ceiling, hearing the sound of the lake, the gentle whine of the wind, and could not sleep.

It was silly not to be able to sleep. Her mother was always saying that . . . *if you want to sleep, Larcy dear, you'll sleep. It's that simple.* . . .

Well, it wasn't that simple, Larcy thought fiercely, no matter how much her mother might claim that it was.

Because she couldn't stop her mind from going around and around, trying to find the end of the maze, trying to fit the pieces of the puzzle together, solving it.

It frightened her. She did not want to puzzle it out, to think about it. She lay in the bed, feeling terribly alone in the big room. The night sounds came in, ominous and brooding, the walls came alive with voiceless murmurings, making her heart pound too fast and the perspiration burst out on her forehead.

She got up finally, tied her robe around her, shoved her feet into the straw sandals she wore on the beach.

Perhaps if she went outside, even took a walk along the beach . . .

She walked slowly, without destination or purpose.

There was no moon, and the stars shone pale and far away, as if shrouded by an invisible gray-black curtain.

The straw sandals made a flopping sound as she walked, but the pounding of the waves against the shore made the sound minute.

She was the only one on the beach. The only one in the whole world. A shiver rippled through her. What a ridiculous, silly thought to have.

"I'll concentrate very hard on deep breathing," she told herself firmly. "I won't allow myself to think of anything else. I'll have a nice glass of warm milk when I get back to the house, and by that time it should be almost twelve-thirty, and I'll give David his injection and then I'll go to bed and I'll sleep beautifully until morning."

She timed herself as she walked . . . Breathe in . . . Hold . . . Exhale . . . Breathe in . . . Hold . . . Exhale . . .

Day after tomorrow would be Thursday. A whole day off. She'd sit in the back yard at home, maybe take her mother uptown for dinner, if she could persuade her to go. And, in spite of what Lyn had told her, it wasn't improbable to think that Pete might be back from Ann Arbor before it was time for her to leave.

She frowned suddenly. Why would Pete be going to Ann Arbor? It was only June. She shrugged. Pete was always having business off somewhere. It needn't have anything to do with the university. He could be seeing about a job for the fall quarter.

Her straw sandals were open at the toes, she

reached down, pulled one off and brushed the sand from between her toes. When she lifted her head she saw the lights of a car a little ways down the beach, where the cutoff led from the highway to Stalen Pier, which was a public fishing spot.

She stood watching idly as a lone figure got out of the car and moved towards the water, dragging something that dragged heavy, like an anchor.

A night fisherman, Larcy thought. She removed her other sandal, cleaned out the sand from between her toes, shook the sandal to free it of sand, and put it back on. It was out of the question to walk farther down the beach dressed in her night clothes.

She knew a moment's irritation. Why did the car have to appear now? Why not later, after she'd finished with her walk and was back at the house?

She shrugged, turned around and headed back for the house, forcing herself to slow, deep breathing.

She warmed herself a glass of milk, drank it slowly, then carefully washed and dried the utensils she had used. She decided to look outside and see if Sybil had set the traps near the garbage containers, but with one hand on the door, she drew back. What if the rat was already in the trap? What would she do? She certainly couldn't kill it. She decided it was best not to know.

A glance at the clock showed five minutes past twelve. No sense in trying to go to sleep for only twenty-five minutes. She lay across the bed in her robe, and determinedly read a short article on soil bacteria. It was incredibly boring and she found her-

107

self yawning before she was half way through it, but she kept reading determinedly. Maybe the real cure for insomnia was boredom.

At twelve-thirty she roused David for his injection. He opened his eyes when she touched his shoulder, protesting he hadn't been asleep, but he *had* been asleep.

He said, "What time's it?"

Larcy told him and he growled, "What're you doing wandering around this time of night?"

"I had to give you your medicine, Mr. Magnam."

"You ain't been to bed yet?" he shot at her.

Larcy said wryly, "Oh, yes, I've been to bed, but I couldn't sleep, so I took a walk along the beach."

There was a sharp snap to his voice. "Who'd you expect to see down there this hour of the night?"

Larcy said patiently, "I didn't expect to see anyone, and I didn't." She didn't mention the car lights she'd seen, the lone figure moving heavily out to the pier. She had forgotten it, except as an annoyance that had sent her scurrying back to the house.

David Magnam's old voice held suspicion. He said, "Nobody goes walking at twelve o'clock at night, unless they've got a reason."

Larcy smoothed the blankets around his shoulders. She said, "But I had a reason, Mr. Magnam, I thought the exercise and the night air would help me to sleep."

Downstairs the telephone rang. The sound startled Larcy. Who would be phoning at twelve-thirty at night? A coldness pushed its way into her bones. Pete.

Pete had gotten himself into a wreck. Someone was calling her about Pete!

She turned, stumbling from the room, down the hall, the stairs, terror riding her. When she reached the downstairs hall, she saw Bena turning from the phone, looking up the stairs at Larcy.

She'd hung up the phone by the time Larcy reached her. She shook her head and said wryly, "Did it startle you, too? I was sleeping so soundly and then the phone rang . . ." She passed a hand across her eyes as if they ached. "I nearly killed myself getting down the stairs. I don't know what I thought . . . perhaps that Johnson's ship had returned earlier than it was supposed to . . ." She shook her head again, "Such silly thoughts we do get, Larcy."

Larcy had stopped her shaking. She said, "I always get frightened when the telephone rings late at night. I can't think of it being anything except bad news."

Bena Pierce laughed sympathetically. "I'm that way about telegrams." She brushed a hand again across her eyes. "It was a wrong number," she said. "It sounded as if the one who was phoning had been drinking." She sighed. "I do hope we'll both be able to get back to sleep again. You'd think people would check the number before phoning, wouldn't you?" She pretended to stifle a yawn.

She switched off the hall light, and followed Larcy up the stairs. "Goodnight, dear," she said, outside the door of her room. She put up a slender hand to her mouth as if to stifle another yawn.

109

"Goodnight," Larcy said. She went down the hall to David Magnam's room, checked the medicine drawer to make certain she'd locked it. She expected David to quiz her about the telephone call, but he was asleep, his mouth open, his breathing coming loud and harsh.

In her own room, Larcy closed the door softly, took off her robe, used a piece of tissue to wipe the sand off her feet, walked to the windows, stared out, took a few deep breaths and climbed into bed.

Bena had been lying. It had not been a wrong number. Larcy had heard the low whisper, heard it distinctly, before Bena had turned and seen Larcy.

Bena had said, "I can't talk now. For God's sake don't phone here again."

The house was old, battered by many winds, pelted by sand storms. It twisted and groaned with age, things moved in the walls. Larcy put her head under the blankets and tried to sleep.

David Magnam picked at his breakfast, finally pushing aside his cereal like a petulant child. "I can't eat that slop," he told Larcy rudely.

Larcy took away the bowl. "I'll bring you something else," she said.

"Don't want anything else," he told her. The folds of flesh under his eyes looked like dark, purplish bruises. He told her to take away the "damned tray and bring me my clipping."

Larcy set the tray off the bed, smoothed the top blanket and brushed the crumbs he'd spilled off onto

110

the floor. She brought him the scrapbook from the table where she'd put it the night before.

"The newspapers are still downstairs," she told him. "I'll bring them up." She picked up the tray.

David Magnam said coldly, "Where's that 'piece of paper,'" his voice mimicked hers, "that you found yesterday?"

Larcy said, "I put it back in the book. You saw me."

He said, "I saw you put the book back on the table, Missy, that's all I saw." His thin, skeleton-like hands were riffling through the heavy scrapbook. He said, looking up at her, as his hands continued to turn the pages, "It ain't here."

Larcy whirled around to stare at him. "Of course it's there," she said. "I'll find it for you." She set the tray down, and took the book from him, looking in the back where she'd stuffed the clipping.

When she failed to find it, she began turning the pages almost desperately. "It's got to be here," she said. "This is where I put it."

But it wasn't there. She said, "Maybe it fell out again." And searched the floor between the table and the bed.

David Magnam watched her. In spite of his weakness there was something almost . . . menacing about him. Larcy looked at his hands, thin, skeleton hands on which the flesh hung, the veins stood out cruelly. But stronger than he let on? Strong enough to use those heavy scissors he was forever cutting with . . . A ball of fear wound and unwound itself inside Larcy.

111

He said coldly, "Seems to me you're sticking your nose into business that don't concern you none. And sometimes when a person does that, they get their nose blown off for their trouble."

Was he threatening her? Fear struggled with indignation. She said, indignation triumphant for the moment, "Mr. Magnam, I don't know what you're suggesting, but I had nothing to do with that clipping falling out. All I did was to pick it up and put it back. And I did put it back, even if it isn't there now."

She stared at him angrily. "Why would I want to keep it? What would I do with it?" She picked up the tray again and went out with it.

The clipping concerned Johnson Pierce. That much certainly seemed obvious. And Bena had taken it? It didn't make sense. If David Magnam already knew who Johnson was, why would the clipping matter?

She passed through the hall into the dining room. Bright morning sunlight sparkled in through the high windows, a slight breeze ruffled the curtains.

Bena, in white slacks and a striped shirt was standing at one of the windows staring out. She turned to greet Larcy, "I was just thinking what a lovely morning it is, Larcy dear." Her eyes were warm and friendly on Larcy's face. "How did you sleep?"

Larcy said, "Like I could have slept longer."

Bena gave a soft laugh. "I know what you mean." She glanced at the tray Larcy carried. "Father eat well this morning?"

Larcy shook her head. Bena's eyes flicked past her to Sybil coming in from the kitchen with a pot of coffee. "What did you leave him doing this morning?" she asked, switching her gaze again to Larcy.

Larcy's hands gripped the tray tighter. She said, trying to keep her voice light, "Being sullen." She smiled. "He can't find a clipping of his. He thinks I neglected to put it in his scrapbook when I picked it up last night.

She did not miss the glance that flashed between Bena Pierce and Sybil. Bena's light laugh sounded forced. She said, "He's behaving very childishly. What earthly reason would you have for keeping his silly old clipping?" She looked at Sybil, frowned. "It could have been picked up by the sweeper. Sybil, did you vacuum upstairs yesterday?"

It seemed for a moment as if the question hadn't gotten through to Sybil, and Bena repeated it, her voice sharpening. "Did you vacuum upstairs yesterday?"

"Yesterday?" Sybil said. She set the coffee pot on the heat pad, frowned down at the table as if concentrating. "Yes," she said, "I did, now I come to think of it." She looked straight at Bena. "Usually I let the upstairs go until Fridays, but I had time yesterday, so I did it early."

"There," Bena said, turning a gentle gaze on Larcy, "that's father's answer, not that he'd believe it, of course. He prefers his own macabre line of reasoning." She stretched out a hand, smoothing a tendril of hair off Larcy's cheek. "Don't give it any more thought, Larcy, dear, father is evidently in one of his moods." She shook her head and her voice sounded sad. "Poor father." She gave a soft laugh. "It wouldn't be a bad

113

idea if more of his clippings disappeared into the sweeper. Gruesome things."

Larcy smiled at her and went on into the kitchen with the tray. Sybil had not vacuumed upstairs yesterday. She was certain of that. Sybil had not known about the clipping until Bena had told her.

She'd lied. They'd both lied. Was the clipping the reason for the blackmail? Did Marian's death have nothing to do with it, after all? A man who had been accused of murder would make a fine suspect for blackmail.

Especially if the person blackmailing him had reason for knowing he should not have been acquitted!

Chapter Twelve

BREAKFAST WAS a slow, pleasant affair. A chipmunk, often a breakfast visitor, perched on the window sill looking in, leaning forward to take the piece of toast Bena brought over to it. "The darling," she said, "isn't it the most adorable darling, Larcy?"

A pair of bronzed grackles searched under the picnic table on the patio for crumbs.

It was a cheerful, peaceful, homey scene, Larcy thought, nothing at all sinister about it. David Magnam would be lying upstairs in his room, probably asleep by now, Lyn was out in the lake having a morning swim, Sybil worked in the kitchen preparing breakfast, across from her sat Bena, sipping at her coffee, looking lovely and tired and kind.

Her voice edged into Larcy's thoughts. She said, "Larcy dear, would you take the car into town for me? There are some errands that must be done this morning and Lyn's gone off, and I have such a horrible headache."

Larcy said, "But Mr. Magnam . . ."

Bena pushed it aside. She said, "You'll be back by lunch time, Larcy, and if he needs anything I can do it for him. Please dear, this is very important to me."

She sounded very insistent, Larcy thought. As insistent as she'd been the day she'd sent Larcy off to the beach. The day she'd met Philip who'd talked to her of blackmail . . . murder.

And then as she looked into Bena's sad, lovely face, saw the deep shadows under her eyes, she hated herself for her suspicions.

"Of course, Mrs. Pierce," she told Bena. "How soon would you want me to leave?"

"As soon as you can get dressed, dear," Bena told her. "That way you'll be back almost before father misses you. Oh, here is our breakfast. Muffins. Isn't this lovely, Larcy? Sybil does make the most delicious muffins, but it isn't often she makes them."

Larcy noticed that Bena, in spite of her words, took only one of the muffins, and she nibbled on that, not quite finishing it.

Lyn came back from her swim just as they were finishing breakfast. She padded barefooted into the dining room, sand encrusted on her slender, tanned legs, on her feet.

She poured herself a cup of coffee, took a muffin, buttered it. She ate standing up, and when Bena suggested, mildly, that it might be better if she showered and dressed, then sat down to eat, she shrugged, said she enjoyed eating standing up, that it was very good for a person's digestion.

She finished the muffin, licked her fingers childishly, then leaned across the table to stare into Bena's face. "I've been reading up on palmistry," she told her. "Let me see your palm, auntie dear."

She pulled Bena's right hand to her and turned it over, palm up. She studied it as if very engrossed in what she was doing. "Well, well," she said, "I see a

116

dark man in your future." She pretended to frown intently. "He seems to be older than you, Bena, and I see him as heavy set, cruel."

Bena pulled back her hand sharply, and then, as if to take away the impact of that, she gave a low, amused laugh. "How very silly," she told Lyn, then switched her gaze to Larcy. "Can you imagine it, some people actually believe in that sort of thing, even pattern their lives after what the lines in their hands or the stars say about them."

"Just the same," Lyn said, giving her a mocking smile, "there's a dark, heavy set man in your future. A person's palm never lies."

She took another muffin, buttered it, and walked out of the dining room eating it.

Bena said slowly, "I try not to mind anything Lyn says. She's very young and she was very fond of my sister, and when Marian died . . ." She veered abruptly away from the subject, "I'll go make a list of the things that need to be done." She got up from her chair, turned her head to watch the chipmunk who, as if suddenly alarmed, slid off the window sill and scurried out of sight. She glanced back at Larcy, smiled. "Don't let me rush you, Larcy, take your time. I have to look up bills and addresses . . ."

"I've finished," Larcy said, "stuffed." She gave a pat little smile and stood up. "I'll take a pitcher of ice water and yesterday's papers upstairs to Mr. Magnam, and then I'll get dressed."

David was lying with his eyes closed when Larcy went into his room. She put the papers on his bed, and set the pitcher of ice water on the stand beside the bed.

117

When she turned around he had opened his eyes and was staring at her. She said, "Would you like to cut now, Mr. Magnam?"

"After a while," he said. "Now don't go taking the stuff off the bed." He narrowed his eyes, the movement contorting his face, so that the wrinkles, the overhanging flesh were like deep, plowed furrows. "You're up to something," he told her, "off somewhere."

"I'm right here," Larcy told him. She decided it wouldn't be wise to tell him Bena had asked her to go into town to do some errands for her.

He changed the subject abruptly. "Whose idea was it to change my medicine? Yours? Bena's?"

Larcy said gently, "It was Dr. Ule's, Mr. Magnam. He thought you'd be more comfortable."

"More comfortable to die, eh?" he said. His eyes narrowed again. "He thinks I'm going to die," he said. "I don't tell him any different. But I'm not going to die. I've got ways . . ." he tapped a forefinger against the side of his head. "It's all in here."

In spite of herself, Larcy shivered. He'd been ill so long, it was pathetic to watch him, listen to him.

He reached a hand under the mattress and brought out the scissors. Larcy watched him cut into the newspaper, in a kind of horrible fascination. It was as if he was cutting into . . . things . . . people.

She drove slowly. She didn't think of herself as a good driver, but she prided herself on being a careful one. The highway was crowded, even at that hour of the morning. She parked in the public park-

118

ing area behind the county-city building, put her money in the meter, then dug into her purse, took out Bena's list and read it.

A book not yet overdue, to be returned to the library, two yards of blue lace, one yard of yellow ribbon, a box of assorted occasion cards, light bulbs from the Edison company, an electric bill.

Larcy slowly tucked the list back in her purse, closed the purse. There was not one thing on Bena's list that needed to be done this particular day.

It took her an hour to finish up Bena's errands. A glance at her watch showed barely ten-thirty. She had a certain feeling that Bena would be annoyed if she returned too soon.

She found a public phone booth and called her mother, and was fiercely disappointed when the phone rang and rang and no one answered. And then she remembered . . . Tuesday was her mother's day for visiting. She made a lark out of it, an occasion.

Sadly Larcy hung up. She'd see her on Thursday, and that was only day after tomorrow. She retrieved her dime from the slot, and then on impulse decided to phone Pete's mother. It could just be that he was already back.

Mrs. Crimmins sounded delighted to hear Larcy's voice. "Your mother was here no more than a half hour ago," she said. "Have you seen her yet?"

And when Larcy said no, she hadn't, Mrs. Crimmins said, "She'll want to see you . . . wait now, I should have the phone number of Ella Adams . . . that's where she was headed . . . wait now . . ."

Larcy said quickly, urgently, "Mrs. Crimmins, I don't have time, I have to be back, I'm just doing some errands for Mrs. Pierce. I'll see mother on Thursday, my day off. I just thought I'd . . ."

The other woman's soft laughter made Larcy blush. "Oh, yes," she said, "yes, of course, you want to talk to Pete." There was apology in her voice. "He's not back from Ann Arbor, Larcy . . ." Her voice held a frown. "He phoned you . . ."

Larcy said, nodding, forgetting the other woman couldn't see the gesture, "I just thought . . . well sometimes Pete changes his mind . . ."

"Not this time," Mrs. Crimmins told her. "He had an appointment to see Mr. Lathrop, of Lathrop, Robbins and Roth, the lawyers, and Pete wouldn't miss a chance like that. He wants to work after class in the law office, he thinks it will be a great chance to learn . . ." She gave a proud laugh. "Pete's so ambitious all of a sudden . . ." There was teasing in her voice, "I wouldn't be at all surprised if you didn't have something to do with it, Larcy."

After Larcy hung up, she decided to buy a couple of books to take back with her, and then have a cool, cool float at one of the drive-ins on her way back to the house.

It was a very small town, mostly a tourist town, and except for the book racks in the drug stores, there was only one book store in the entire town.

Larcy bought only one book, and she wasn't particularly enthusiastic about it, but it would give her something with which to occupy herself when the fog or the rain closed in.

120

She had the book and the parcels containing Bena's purchases under one arm, and she swung her purse back and forth in her other hand as she walked.

She had a habit of glancing into store windows as she passed, restaurants . . . you never could know when you might see a particular hat or dress you simply had to own, or a friend in one of the restaurants or soda fountains.

She glanced casually in at the steam tables and the same perspiring man in the same dirty apron she and Pete had seen that Thursday in the Coney Island.

She could not believe her eyes when she saw Bena Pierce sitting at the counter, her face turned away from the street, seemingly engaged in a very serious discussion with a thin faced, dark haired, very untidy, very prepossessing young man whose face was turned so that his features were quite visible to Larcy.

Larcy became aware after a second that she was staring. The cook, evidently thinking she was struck by admiration of his prowess, winked at her, and deftly turned one of the hot dogs simmering on the grill.

Larcy shifted her parcels, quickly averted her face, and began walking. It could not have been Bena Pierce. She'd left Bena at the house, she had Bena's car.

And besides, it was incredible to think of the fastidious, lovely Bena sitting in such an unlikely place, and with such an unlikely escort.

Larcy shook her head, as if trying to shake away

121

what she had seen. She walked to the parking lot, unlocked the car, put her parcels in the back seat, and carefully backed the car out.

She had been mistaken, she told herself. She'd only thought it was Bena . . . after all, she hadn't seen her face, had she? And was Bena Pierce the only woman with black hair, who wore it in that particular style? Or the only woman partial to yellow?

And besides, if Bena had been coming into town herself, would she have sent Larcy in to do her errands for her?

No, of course not. So, it just had to be a case of mistaken identity. Still Larcy frowned, wanting to believe it, but not quite able to convince herself.

Bena could have taken the bus into town, she could have met someone and driven in with them. *But why send me away then,* Larcy thought, *on a trumped up errand?*

It didn't make sense . . . it didn't make sense at all. If Bena had wanted to get Larcy out of the house for a couple of hours, why then would she go into town?

It began to look like an unsolvable puzzle. Unless . . . Larcy's spine began to tingle . . . Unless something had come up to interfere with whatever plans Bena had contemplated. Something . . . Someone . . .

And what plans did she think Bena had contemplated, for heaven's sake? She was irritable with herself. She was forever making mysteries out of the commonplace.

It was none of her business, none at all, where Bena

Pierce went or whom she met. Mrs. Pierce was her employer. It was not her job to pry into her private life.

Unless it concerned her patient's safety. And did it concern her patient's safety? That tingle began again riding up and down Larcy's spine. Could the man she'd seen with Bena be the second blackmailer? What was it she'd heard Bena say that day when she'd been trapped on the hill, forced into listening? . . . *Someone else knows? You told someone else?* . . .

Larcy kept her hands firmly on the wheel on the drive back. What was it she was afraid of? . . . That someone was planning to . . . murder David Magnam?

It was a ridiculous thought. The bright, sunshiny day, the laughing people in open cars heading for the beach all pointed to the ridiculousness of it. She did not stop for the float at the drive-in.

Bena was not at home when Larcy got there. She tried not to think of the significance of it. She put her purchases on the dining room table and went up to her room to change into her uniform.

The house was curiously quiet, empty, forbidding. Larcy changed quickly, as if haste was necessary, and hurried down the silent hall to David Magnam's room.

He turned a sullen gaze on her as she walked over to the bed. "You're being paid a salary to take care of me," he told her, "my needs, not to run errands for her. Don't forget where your salary's coming from. *My* money."

So Bena had told him after all, Larcy thought. She fluffed up his pillow, smoothed his bed, felt the side of his water pitcher. "You need fresh ice water," she told him. "I'll bring you some."

She picked up the water pitcher and was aware of David Magnam's eyes fixed steadily on her face. He said, "She went someplace, someplace she was in a hurry to get to. I heard her, racing around, getting her things on, running down the stairs like the devil himself was after her." He gave a dry, mirthless laugh, "maybe he was."

Larcy said, "I'll get the water." He let her go. She walked slowly along the hall, down the stairs. Sunlight filtered in, turning the grains of sand that always littered the floor into sparkling diamonds.

It had been Bena Pierce she'd seen, no use in trying to talk herself out of it. It had been Bena.

Sybil was not in the kitchen. The house held the feel of loneliness, of emptiness. How long had he been left alone? And for what purpose?

Larcy's hands were as cold as the ice cubes she dropped into the water pitcher. She did not like the way things were beginning to look, she did not like it at all.

If only Pete were here . . . somebody she could trust. Feeling gloomy and depressed, she went out of the kitchen. She encountered Lyn flying in the door, flashing a newspaper above her head.

"Excitement at last," she squealed. "There's been a murder off Stalen Pier!"

124

Chapter Thirteen

LARCY'S HEART thudded; she felt strangely light headed. If it wasn't for the coldness of the pitcher against her hands, she could almost force herself to believe it wasn't happening.

"It was a man," Lyn went on, her eyes shining, as if she were truly excited. "The police found his body this morning stuffed into a rowboat . . ." her brown eyes were suddenly avid on Larcy's face, "say," she said, "say . . . you look like you're going to be sick . . . Larcy Ryan . . . one would almost think you knew something about the murder!"

Knew something about the murder? Larcy stared at her tormentor with sick, frightened eyes. *Stalen Pier . . . Stalen Pier . . . it was here she had seen the lights last night!*

She ran her tongue over her dry, tight lips. *And the lone figure dragging something heavy. Like an anchor,* Larcy had thought. But it hadn't been an anchor . . . it had been a body . . . a *dead* body . . .

The somber, silent house seemed to hold an air of sinister listening. Larcy shuddered thinking of what could have happened if she hadn't seen the lights in time, or if she'd decided to go on and have her walk, and the heck with it. What if she had disturbed the . . . murderer? Would she have . . . joined that other body in the rowboat?

Lyn leaned towards Larcy. She said, "you look frightened to death. I'm not at all frightened . . . I think it's exciting . . . I'm not at all upset because it happened so close to here." Her eyes narrowed, became veiled. She said, softly, slyly, "Aunt Bena wasn't in her room last night, did you know that, Larcy?"

Larcy shook her head, and Lyn said slowly, "No, of course you wouldn't know it, because you weren't in your room, either, Larcy."

Larcy almost spoke . . . *"How do you know this? Because you sneak around, slip into other people's rooms, spy on them?"* Instead, she said carefully, "I couldn't sleep last night. I took a walk. I was back shortly after midnight. I stayed up until twelve-thirty when I had to give Mr. Magnam his injection."

Lyn said, oh so carefully, "It says here that the police believe the man was killed around eleven-thirty or thereabouts. It's a good thing, Larcy, that you don't have to produce an alibi, you or Aunt Bena."

Larcy pretended to find it a joke, and said with a light laugh, "And you, Lyn? Would you have an alibi?"

"Me?" Lyn said loudly. "For heaven's sake, Larcy, why would I need an alibi? Why should anyone in this house need an alibi? Who do we know who's short, dark, middle aged and . . . dead?" She turned her head, looked behind her, and said, as if totally surprised, "Why, Aunt Bena, I didn't know you were standing there listening."

126

But she had known, Larcy thought. It was why she had raised her voice, said what she had.

Bena's smoky eyes looked sick, and there was a grayish cast to her usually shining, clear complexion. "You're back, Larcy? I . . ." She shook her head.

She'd been going to tell some story, Larcy thought, of where she had been, and then had decided against telling it. She turned her gaze on Lyn.

Her voice, her eyes were meant to give the impression of bewilderment. "What are you talking about? Who is dead?"

"Who?" Lyn repeated the question carefully. "I don't know, the newspaper doesn't know, the police don't know. All they know for sure, is that he's very dead. Shot someplace else they think, and brought to Stalen Pier in a car."

She was looking directly at Bena, her young face smug, mocking. "They . . . the police . . . think the killer was frightened away by something . . . somebody . . . before he could properly dispose of the body."

The brown eyes raked Bena's pale face. "It says *he* in the newspaper, but that isn't what it means. Not really. The police think a woman . . . could have done it. The body was dragged, you see. There were drag marks on the sand."

Larcy's voice came out, too loud, fear tinged, she said slowly, heavily, "Last night . . . when I was taking a walk. . . . I saw car lights down there . . ." She licked her dry lips, looked frantically at Bena Pierce, "I had on my night clothes . . . I

127

thought it was a fisherman . . . I wasn't dressed to see anybody, so I turned around and came back."

Lyn whistled. She said, "Imagine that. If you'd been seen . . ." There was an edge of mockery to her words. "Why Larcy, you might even be dead by now."

Larcy shuddered, and Bena said, without looking at Lyn, "Stop such talk. It's a terrible way to talk. Can't you see she's frightened to death even thinking about it?"

Her voice dropped a note, "Larcy," she said, "think, dear, it could be very important to the police . . . it could even be . . . dangerous for you . . . are you sure . . . very sure . . . that you did not see the person who . . . did it? You couldn't . . . recognize him?"

Lyn cut in smoothly, "Or her, Larcy."

Bena ignored her, keeping her gaze intent on Larcy. Larcy shook her head. "No," she said, "no. It was too far away, and it was dark. I couldn't tell for sure even whether it was a man or a woman." She looked miserably at Bena, licked her dry lips again. "Perhaps," she said, "I should say something to the police? It could be important . . . the time element, I mean."

Lyn's mocking voice cut in. "But of course you should, Larcy. It's your civic duty, didn't you know that?"

Larcy, getting hold of herself, calmer now, frowned in her direction. "I don't think that . . . murder . . . is anything to make a joke about."

It was Bena who said quietly, "Of course it isn't,

128

and of course you should tell the police whatever you know."

Were the smoky eyes regarding Larcy in apprehension? Larcy looked down at the water pitcher she was holding. "Oh," she said, "I have to take this up to Mr. Magnam." She looked again at Bena, said, "I put your things and the money left over, on the dining room table."

Bena's eyes held hers. She said, with a soft sigh, "I don't know why I thought those things had to be done this morning. I guess I thought the library book was overdue . . . they do make such a fuss about an overdue book." She gave a little laugh. "But at least it's off my mind now, I won't worry about it." She shook her head, turned to gaze outside at the wealth of blue sky, white sand, and blue-green lake calm and serene this morning. "Why would anyone want to do violence to someone else?" she asked thoughtfully.

Still shaking her head she went through the hall into the dining room beyond.

Larcy, walking slowly up the stairs remembered unhappily that Bena had replied to David Magnam's taunt that she could get his money if she killed him, by saying, *don't think I haven't thought of it.*

Was what she had said now a contradiction? Larcy frowned, and her hand tightened around the handle of the water pitcher. People, the nicest of people, sometimes thought in terms of violence when they were angry and upset. But that did not mean they had any intention of committing violence.

She set the water pitcher on the bedside table

where David Magnam could reach it. She was very careful not to mention the murder that had occurred last night.

She busied herself straightening up his room, opening the curtains, throwing up the blinds, letting sunshine and the fresh, clean lake air into the room.

He did look better, she thought. The increased medication was good for him, he seemed to be in no pain at all. She turned her head and ooked out over the lake.

Such a lovely day, she thought, a day for relaxing in the sun, for being well and alive, for laughing. And yet, here in this room David Magnam was slowly dying, and in the morgue in town, an unknown man lay dead of violence.

She shivered, and the breeze sifting in through the screened windows seemed hot and dry and uncomfortable. The lake water would be cold, and the sun too hot on one's back.

It was two o'clock when the detective came. "I phoned him, Larcy," Bena told her. "I said you had something to tell him about the murder."

"Oh," Larcy said. And waited, and stared at the tall, fair, boyish looking man who had risen from the tan sofa when she had come into the room.

"This is Lieutenant Carey Bricker," Bena said, "he's from the Port Hope police." She was wearing yellow silk slacks and a white blouse piped in yellow. Her smoky eyes were shadowed and lines of fatigue dragged down the corners of her mouth.

Larcy was not prepared for a detective who looked

as boyish and brash as Pete, and nearly as young. She felt a pang of doubt. A detective should be older, dignified, stern visaged . . .

But after a few moments she knew that the boyishness, the brashness, was merely a front, and this man knew his job very well. She thought that she could be glad she was not a criminal being hunted by him.

The living room was bright, sunshiny and comfortably untidy. He seemed to be completely at ease as he smiled down at her and said, "Mrs. Pierce says you saw someone down at Stalen Pier last night. While you were taking a walk around midnight." His lips pursed, his eyes held a flicker of cold amusement as if he did not believe she'd been taking a walk at all.

Larcy's eyes flashed, she forgot to be in awe of him. She said crisply, coldly, "I *was* taking a walk . . . I couldn't sleep and I had to be up at 12:30 to give my patient his medicine. After an hour of rolling and tossing, I got up, put on my robe and sandals and walked along the beach. And I saw the car lights . . ."

Her voice caught in her throat and she looked up at him miserably, remembering what could have happened to her. She shook her head, said in a small, tight voice, "If I'd bothered to get dressed, I'd have kept on walking, but I wasn't dressed, so I came back to the house." She looked down at her hands. She was holding them clasped in front of her. They were shaking.

He said smoothly, "About what time would you say this was?"

131

Larcy shook her head. "It was five minutes after twelve when I got back to my room."

"You saw a man?" he persisted.

Larcy shook her head again. "Not a man," she said. "A figure. The figure . . . person . . . seemed to be dragging something heavy. I thought it was a fisherman . . . that he was dragging an anchor." She began to shiver. "That's all I can tell you . . . that's all I saw."

In spite of her denials that she'd seen anything else, he persisted in asking her about what she had seen, over and over. When she protested that she'd told him everything, the first time he'd asked her, he said smoothly that sometimes, in repeating a story, a person added or subtracted certain details. He looked down at her, said grudgingly, "You did neither."

Lyn, who'd been an interested listener, asked, "Do you know who he is? The one who was murdered?"

"Not yet," he told her. "But we're working on something. We'll find out."

Did his eyes rest too long on Bena Pierce's face? Larcy silently shook herself. What a silly thought to have. Why would he think Bena would have any knowledge of who the murdered man was?

He took his leave, and Larcy, on her way to the kitchen, heard Lyn's voice, softly insinuating, say, "I warned you there was a dark, heavy set man in your future, auntie dear."

Larcy did not hear Bena's reply. In the kitchen Sybil had a stool drawn up to an open window, and was scraping carrots.

132

She turned her head when Larcy came into the room, an unprecedented act of interest for Sybil. She asked harshly, "What's he doing here?"

"He's from the police department," Larcy told her. "Mrs. Pierce told him that I'd seen some lights down at Stalen Pier last night."

"And did you?" Sybil asked.

"Yes," Larcy nodded. "Car lights."

"And what else did you see?" Sybil's glance was knife sharp on Larcy's face.

"Nothing," Larcy told her. "Just the car lights and a figure."

"Man or woman?" Sybil asked.

"I don't know," Larcy told her. "It was dark, and I was too far away."

Sybil said, "Just as well you didn't see too much. Less dangerous."

Larcy poured herself a glass of ice water from the refrigerator, and walked outside to the patio with it, startling a ground squirrel digging under the picnic table.

Bena had known about the murder when she'd returned from town. Why had she pretended not to know? She'd known, and was frightened. Something unbidden popped into Larcy's mind, Philip Francis was short, dark, middle aged. And Lyn had said, *there's going to be a dark, heavy set man in your future* . . . How had she known?

And did she also know something about the murder? Something she had neglected to tell the detective?

133

Out on the lake a warning bell sounded from one of the freighters. Why a warning bell? Larcy wondered. It was a clear, bright day, not a sign of fog.

But then, the bell could also sound as a greeting when passing another ship. She ran a hand over the smooth, varnished top of the picnic table. She was filled with nervousness, apprehension. She wished Pete was back . . . that she could talk to him.

She walked slowly back inside the house. Lyn, still in her bathing suit, was standing in the hall staring outside. She turned around and looked gleefully at Larcy. She said, "Do you think, Larcy, that whoever did it, thinks maybe you did see them, and will come back to kill you, so you won't be able to tell anyone?"

Larcy stared at her in horror. She said fiercely, "That's perfectly silly. You read too many of those ridiculous detective stories, see too much Hitchcock on TV . . . besides," she stared steadily at Lyn, "I didn't see anyone."

Chapter Fourteen

THE SOUND echoed and re-echoed through the hall, digging with piercing fingers past Larcy's door, into her consciousness.

She opened her eyes, stared groggily into the darkness of her bedroom. The smell of damp and cold crept in through the opened windows.

She'd been dreaming, a nightmare. She pressed her fingers against her temples, and then the sound came again, strangled, horrible, a sound without words, the desperate, frantic attempt of somebody to make themselves heard, and without a voice in which to call out.

Larcy was never to remember getting up, making her way along the dark hallway, its silence no longer broken by the sound that had stopped now.

The night lay outside, silent and dark and cold. The door to David Magnam's room was closed— and it should not have been closed. She'd left it open. She always left it open.

The night light was burning as she'd left it when she'd looked in on him at ten-thirty. She switched on the overhead light, flooding the room with brightness.

Her patient's eyes were open, but he did not seem to see her, his breathing was loud and uneven, his pulse ragged.

When Larcy looked up, Bena was standing in the doorway, looking sleepy eyed, frightened, bewildered.

"What's happened to father?" She put one slender hand against her mouth, pressing her lips inward. "I heard this awful sound . . ."

Her eyes sought Larcy's. She said, "Is he . . . dead?"

Larch shook her head, said quietly, "I think you'd better call the doctor."

Bena stared at her, and then, as if suddenly becoming completely awake, her feet flew towards the door.

Before she reached the hall, Lyn came stumbling out of her room, to stand in the doorway staring in. "What's all the excitement?" she asked. "Someone else get murdered? I hope."

Bena said fiercely, "Can't you see he's in a bad way? And don't make a joke about it. Have some respect for his age and illness, at least."

Lyn said softly, "Don't get your hopes up too high, Bena dear. He *isn't* dead yet. He'll probably outlive all of us, out of spite."

A mocking note came into her voice, "Unless someone . . . helps him to die, that is." She flung a glance at the bed, "and maybe someone has decided to do just that."

The overhead light fell directly on Bena's face, and Larcy thought that she looked tired, tired and . . . old. She'd never before thought of the word in connection with Bena. It gave her a feeling of pity for the other woman.

Not by so much as a tightening of her lips did

136

Bena let on that she'd heard Lyn's words. At the head of the stairs, Larcy saw her hand grip the newel post and then descend slowly.

She heard the slam of the door as Lyn went back into her own room. Larcy bent over David Magnam, held his arms when he threshed wildly, wiped the thin beads of cold sweat from his forehead.

Bena came softly back into the room. She said, "he'll be here as soon as he can make it." She stared unhappily down at her father. "He's dying," she said. "How can you stand there doing nothing? You'd think you'd give him something . . . let him die in peace . . . not this way."

Larcy said, "I'm only a nurse, Mrs. Pierce. I can't prescribe. Only a doctor can do that."

Bena said bitterly, frantically, "Why doesn't he get here?"

They crowded the bedroom, that was not overly large, Bena, the doctor, Larcy, Sybil standing in the doorway, silent, watching. Only Lyn was conspicuous by her absence.

The doctor, his eyes red rimmed, his thin face looking scooped out, frowned, ignored everyone except Larcy and his patient. When he looked over David Magnam's head at Larcy, she could see it in his eyes, he did not expect that David was going to live out the night.

And then suddenly, miraculously, he took a turn for the better. He'd been given a drug to slow down the terrible pounding of his heart, to steady his pulse, and . . . it was working. She saw the smile on the doctor's face as he lifted his head, replaced his stethoscope.

"I'll give him something to keep him asleep," he told Larcy. "He shouldn't be left alone . . ." He glanced around the room. "Is there any way you could have a cot brought in?"

Bena said, "Of course, there's a cot upstairs in the attic. We can bring it down."

Larcy shook her head. "There's a chair in my room," she said, "quite a comfortable one. I can bring that in here. I wouldn't be at all comfortable falling asleep."

Bena said, "I'll take my turn at sitting up with him . . ." and then at Larcy's look, she appealed to the doctor, "Tell her. I insist. After all he is my father and besides . . ." she flung a soft, gentle glance at Larcy, and then turned her charm on the doctor, "it will be much better for father if his nurses are fresh and wide awake." She turned her eyes on Larcy again, "I know you tell yourself you won't get sleepy, or go to sleep, but Larcy, that's a human impossibility," she swung her gaze back on the doctor, "tell her."

He smiled and said, "Not an impossibility, my dear Bena, but doctors and nurses are only human after all, and we do get sleepy." He glanced down at his watch, "let her spell you off, Larcy," he told her, "she wants to, and it will probably be good for her, keep her from worrying."

He patted Bena's shoulder. "He pulled through tonight," he said, "but one of these days . . ." he sighed, "my dear, you have to accept the fact of his dying."

138

Bena put up a slender hand as if to ward off his words. "But not like tonight," she said, "it was. . . . horrible to watch. Wasn't there anything she . . . could have given him?" She flung her hands outward in an apologetic motion as she looked unhappily at Larcy, "I'm not criticizing you, my dear, I'm just . . . wondering, so that if . . . something like this happens again . . ."

Larcy flushed. The doctor said slowly, carefully, "Miss Ryan used very good judgment in not giving him the morphine. It could have been dangerous."

He frowned, as he snapped shut his bag, lifted it. "Tonight," he said, "was caused by overexcitement, and there should be no more of it. In his condition . . ." he shook his head, frowned down at the figure lying quiet and still on the bed.

"Overexcitement?" Larcy stared at Bena, at the doctor. She said, "But Dr. Ule, there was nothing unusual. He had his supper, did some clipping for his scrapbook, had his injection at eight-thirty. At ten-thirty when I looked in on him before going to bed, he was asleep. Everything was quiet . . . it was the same as on any other day."

The doctor shrugged, looked puzzled. "It could have been something else," he said. "In cases like his, well, a doctor can't always know for sure what will bring on an attack."

Bena went downstairs with him. Sybil moved into the room. She said, "I'll help you move that chair in here." She stepped off briskly.

Larcy followed her, slowly, engrossed in deep

thinking. She'd said there'd been nothing unusual, but there had been. The murder.

Inside her room, with Sybil on one side of the chair and her on the other, she asked carefully, "Did anyone bring this afternoon's newspaper up to Mr. Magnam?"

Sybil began shaking her head, in that blank fashion, and then her head snapped up. She said, "Yes . . . now I think of it, Lyn took it up to him."

"After I went to bed?" Larcy asked, slowly, quietly.

Sybil shook her head, retreating. "I wouldn't know what time it was. I saw her with the paper, and she said she was going to take it up to him."

Larcy's face tightened. She said, "And you didn't stop her?"

Sybil's flat, dull face sharpened. She said, "Why would I stop her? He's always reading about murders . . . hasn't he got a whole scrapbook about them?"

"But not," Larcy thought, "about a murder committed no farther than Stalen Pier." She frowned. Still, Sybil was right. Why would another murder more or less excite a man like David Magnam? *Unless . . .* that ball of fear was churning around in her stomach again, *unless he . . . knew the murder victim . . . or . . . something about the murder.*

Larcy, sitting in the chair Sybil had helped her bring into David Magnam's room, closed her eyes. The clock on the stand by the bed had said ten minutes past two, the last time she'd looked at it.

140

Her eyes felt heavy, weighed down. The room, the hall outside the half opened door had taken on a curiously pregnant silence. It was as if the very silence carried a threat that invaded everything, drifting into the shadows, settling in the very walls.

Something caught in Larcy's throat, and she opened her eyes, turned her head slowly, feeling with an unreasoning sense of panic, a shrinking of her bones, that something had moved out there in the darkened hall. Something . . . Someone.

She heard the loud, harsh sound of David Magnam's breathing, the ticking of the clock, so loud in the silence. What else had she heard? Nothing, of course. There was nothing.

Still she listened, tensed, hardly breathing, poised for flight. And saw Lyn's pajama clad figure appearing suddenly in the doorway, pushing the door open farther, stepping inside the room, advancing to stand in front of Larcy, eyes mocking in the dim, yellowish night light, hands posed dramatically on slender hips.

"You look as if you were expecting to see a ghost," she said, in a light, mocking whisper. "Larcy, you do look so . . . scared." The brown eyes lit with wild amusement. "Maybe you thought that person . . . the one who murdered that man . . . had come after you. Is that what you were thinking, Larcy?"

Larcy said, keeping her voice calm with an effort, "I dozed off for a minute. It was like coming out of a dream." She changed tactics, asked a question of her own, "What are you doing here?" She threw the last word in deliberately, "now?"

Lyn said slowly, "you thought I should have been in here when Dr. Ule was here. That's what you're implying, isn't it? I'm no hypocrite like the rest of them. Why should I pretend I'd be sorry? I won't be. He's a mean, miserable, vindictive old man. His being sick doesn't change one thing."

She gave her head a quick toss. "I didn't give him yesterday's newspaper, I heard Sybil tell you I did . . . I was going to, and then I didn't. . . . I thought of something else to do, I guess. But somebody took the paper . . . It wasn't on the dining room table when I went back to get it."

Somebody else had taken the newspaper? Somebody who wanted . . . or didn't want . . . David Magnam to read it?

Lyn inclined her head towards the bed. "I'm not sorry," she said, "about him. Oh, he won't die, not for a long, long time. He's too mean, too miserable. He'll live and have a good laugh over other people choking to death waiting for him to die."

She whirled and went out of the room again, closing the door behind her, as she always did. With a sigh, Larcy got up, pushing her wooden feet along the floor, opening the door, so that the light from the room lit a small portion of the darkness outside the door.

She looked down on her patient, listening to his breathing, timing his pulse, her skillful fingers finding the faint beat, pushing aside the folds of loose skin that hung from the thin wrists.

It was four o'clock when Bena came to relieve her. She said, apologetically, "I fell asleep, Larcy, I

142

didn't think I would. Did you think I was never coming?"

"Mrs. Pierce," Larcy said, "did you give him yesterday's newspaper?"

"Yesterday's newspaper?" Bena frowned, slowly shook her head. "No . . . no I don't remember doing it . . . I saw it there and at first I thought of doing it and then . . . well, I decided it might not be a good thing . . . the murder being so near us and all." The smoky eyes searched Larcy's face. "Do you think . . . Larcy, surely not the murder of that man . . . why what would it mean to father? Just another act of violence for that scrapbook of his."

Larcy said slowly, "I don't know what I think. But Dr. Ule said something overexcited him. What else was there, except the murder? The headlines in the paper?"

Bena appeared to consider it. Frowning she glanced down at the figure of her father lying so quietly in the big bed. "But . . ." she said, "whatever would he know about it? The police don't even know who the man is."

Larcy stared hollowly at Bena, her mind going around and around, puzzling, trying to sort things out, put the pieces together . . . "I'm tired," she thought, "too tired . . . too tired." She passed a hand wearily over her forehead. "I'll go lie down now," she said. "If he wakes up, if there's any change, any change at all, call me."

"Yes," Bena said. She leaned over her father, said, her voice a whisper, "He's sleeping, he doesn't seem to be in any pain now."

"He isn't in pain," Larcy told her. She moved towards the door as Bena sank down into the arm chair. "Remember," Larcy cautioned her, "any change."

Bena nodded. "I won't go to sleep," she said. She stretched her arms high above her head, stifled a yawn, said softly, "What did Lyn want, Larcy?"

What did Lyn want? Bena said she'd been asleep. If she had been asleep, how did she know Lyn had been in the room? How would she know that unless she'd been outside in the hall, seen Lyn come into the room?

Larcy felt the cold perspiration bathe the insides of her palms. "Lyn?" she said. "She just wanted to know how Mr. Magnam was."

She didn't want to tell her Lyn had come to tell her about the newspaper, that she hadn't given it to Mr. Magnam, that it wasn't where she'd left it. She didn't want to tell Bena because she was afraid.

The roof of her mouth felt hot and dry. It was safer to say nothing, see nothing, do nothing. A coldness pressed against her spine. Perhaps she should have talked more to Lt. Bricker. *And told him what?* her mind chided her. *The quarrel between Bena and her father? The talk she'd overheard between Bena and the man she'd called "Phil"? the poison Sybil was supposed to have burned in the fireplace along with the rat? Supposed to have burned, because Larcy did not believe Sybil had caught a rat? The thing Lyn had said about there being a dark, heavy set man in Bena's future?*

And if she had done that, involved them all,

144

would she solve the murder at Stalen Pier? Save David Magnam from being murdered? Or would she solve nothing, except to throw suspicion on people on whom there should be no suspicion?

She paused in the doorway, "the doctor said it could have been caused by anything," she said. She pushed a smile onto her dry lips. "The thing is," she said, "he's pulled through it."

Bena's sigh seemed to shake her slender body. She said, her voice a low, taut whisper, "For now, Larcy, for now."

Larcy moved quickly down the dark hall, glad when she reached her own room, and could shut and lock the door. Through the opened windows she could hear the water lapping gently, monotonously at the sand.

Had there been a warning in Bena's words? A threat? *Nonsense*, she told herself firmly, there had been neither. Only the unhappy, dreary acceptance of death to someone very close, even if that someone was neither loved, wanted, nor accepted.

Chapter Fifteen

THURSDAY was a day of gray, sullen skies, strong gusts of damp laden winds, and fog that rose from the bottoms and shrouded the branches of the trees and lay like a thick, uneven carpet across the roads.

David Magnam had seemed quite pleased by the sensation he'd caused. "Fooled them, didn't I?" he gloated to Larcy. "Thought I was a goner, didn't you? Bena probably shed a lot of tears, for Ule's benefit, for yours, make you think she wouldn't be glad." His eyes, faded, dulled by months of illness, glared venomously into Larcy's, "I'm not going to die," he said. Once again, he tapped a forefinger against the side of his head. "It's all in here," he told her, "I've got ways of cheating death."

Larcy knew it was only a feeble defiance, that no one had the power of cheating death, but even knowing it, she felt depressed, fearful.

She'd brought him up Wednesday's paper, but Tuesday's paper with its grisly headlines was not to be found, and the front page was gone from Wednesday's paper.

He'd snapped viciously at her, "Whose idea is it that I'm to get my newspaper with half of it gone?" His eyes narrowed on her face, "What was there in the paper I wasn't to see?"

Larcy shook her head. She said, "It wasn't that, Mr. Magnam, I'm sure. Sybil wraps the garbage in

146

newspaper, she puts newspaper on the kitchen floor after she scrubs. If no other paper was handy, she might have picked up today's paper and used it, not thinking."

He said, "And yesterday's paper? She'd have used that, too?"

Larcy shook her head, "I don't know, Mr. Magnam."

But this morning he'd grinned at her in apparent glee. "So we've got a murder?" he said. His thin lips twisted at one corner. He said, "I've got a radio, evidently everyone forgot that."

Larcy merely nodded, said nothing. In less than an hour she'd be out of the house, on her way home. There was a fierce want in her for the normalcy of her mother, the kitchen with its smell of food cooking, the sometimes intolerable heat of the small living room. Her mother was always forgetful about turning on the window fan Larcy had bought for her.

David Magnam glared at her. He said, looking as if he was enjoying himself, "I know who he is."

Larcy stared at him. "The murderer?"

He gave his head an exasperated shake. "I'll know that after I do some thinking about it," he told her. "I'm talking about the victim. I know who he is."

He leaned back into the pillows, looking excessively pleased with himself.

Larcy said quietly, "Then you should tell the police, Mr. Magnam. It will save them a lot of work." Her eyes searched his face. "Besides," she told him, "it's against the law to hold back information."

David gave that sharp, dry laugh of his, that was

147

more like a bark. "What law?" he asked her. "You tell them I know who he is, I'll say different."

Larcy said, shrugging, "you probably don't know who he is, Mr. Magnam. You're just wanting to say something."

If she thought her words would arouse him, she was mistaken. He just continued to look smug and said, "Oh, I know who he is, all right."

And Larcy, looking at him, knew somehow, with a dread certainty, that he spoke the truth.

The bus drive home was unpleasant. The tires swished on the wet pavement, the bus skidded once too close to an embankment, lights came at them dimly out of the fog, unreal, gloomy, depressing.

It was raining when the bus pulled into the station, a chilling, misty vapor of rain. Larcy had no desire to wait in the rain for a city bus. She phoned a cab and waited on one of the hard benches in the bus station.

She remembered sitting with Pete on the same hard bench, how long ago? Only a week? She dug restlessly in her purse, found a mirror, gazed at her reflection, put the mirror away, closed her purse.

Wouldn't Pete be back by now? If he was, then why hadn't he phoned her? She could see the bus driver at the snack bar, lighting a cigarette. She wondered if he got nervous driving the bus, worried. She thought of the return trip. She wouldn't wait until eight tonight, unless it cleared up. She'd go back early, before dark.

At the thought of going back there, depression

148

settled over her. If Pete was back, he'd drive her. Pete was a lousy driver, but she wasn't afraid driving with Pete. She'd never been afraid.

Why hadn't Pete phoned her if he was back from Ann Arbor? A small stab of doubt pushed its way into her mind. Maybe he'd found another girl.

Her mind rejected the thought, quickly and decisively. Pete and she belonged together . . . they'd both of them always more or less taken it for granted.

But the status quo could change any time. Pete could fall in love, really in love, with some girl. She could fall madly in love with someone else.

She thought sadly of how badly her mother would feel if something like that was to happen. The taxi arrived and she scooped up her gloves and bag and walked out through the glass doors to where it waited at the curb.

Pete was not going to fall in love with anyone else, she was not going to fall in love with anyone else.

The traffic along the street moved slowly, sometimes it was almost as if they were standing still.

"Paper says it's going to clear by afternoon." The driver vouchsafed the information, throwing it back at Larcy.

"It can stand clearing," Larcy said. There was nothing to see out of the window except the fog and the yellow lights coming at them, moving past them.

She closed her eyes, and a small frown cut across her forehead. It was odd, wasn't it odd, how much she seemed to be thinking of Pete lately?

She tucked the thought in the back recesses of her mind, to be pondered over later.

She leaned forward and touched the driver on one shoulder, "That's my street coming up next," she told him.

He nodded, not turning his head. "Lady," he said, "I was born and lived in this town all of my life. I don't think there's a street, old or new, that I don't know about or been on. I used to think of going off, trying my luck in a bigger town." His shrug was eloquent. "I got tied down with a wife and a kid before I was out of high school, and I'm too old to leave now." He turned the corner a bit too sharp, and Larcy held onto the door handle to keep from falling sideways.

"Took that one a bit sharp," he said. He swung down the street, to stop in front of the white frame house that Larcy pointed out.

She paid him, and allowed a generous tip. She felt sorry for him, really sorry. It wasn't that she didn't love Port Hope, because she did, but to never be able to leave it and try your wings someplace else . . . to be so loaded down with family and responsibility . . .

Pete and she would leave. Her mother would be sad . . . a little. Pete's mother would be sad . . . a little. But they'd leave. They'd come back from time to time, because it was home and it housed those they loved, but not to stay. Never to stay.

Thinking about it made her sad, as if by the very act of contemplating living someplace else, she was throwing aside the shackles of girlhood, emerging, transforming . . . and she wasn't at all sure she wanted to throw off the shackles . . . they were so comforting, so secure . . . so . . . there.

Her mother had been waiting, timing the exact hour she'd reach the house. Larcy could tell by the way the door was flung open and her mother was out on the porch before she had reached the top step.

She put her arms around Larcy and kissed her soundly and then stepped back and said, chidingly, "You didn't tell me you were going to come in on Tuesday."

Larcy laughed and leaning forward, kissed her. "I didn't tell you for the reason that I didn't know it myself until that morning." She took her mother's arm, "Let's go inside, it's miserable and nasty out here."

She sniffed as she stepped inside. "Sauce for spaghetti and meat balls," she moaned. "Mother, you're just trying to get me fat."

"Sit down in the living room," her mother told her, "and I'll bring in a pitcher of iced tea. I fixed it the way you like it, with those bits of orange and lemon slices floating around in it." She gave her daughter a smug smile, "I remembered to turn on the fan too," she told her.

Larcy laughed and said wryly, "Of course you'd remember, mother, my darling, on a day when we won't need the fan."

But she took her mother's advice, sat down, kicked off her shoes, and tucked her feet under her. She looked around when her mother came in, bearing a tray on which rested a pitcher of iced tea, two glasses, and a plate of cookies.

151

"I shouldn't let you wait on me," Larcy told her mother, reaching for one of the cookies, and pouring herself a glass of tea with the other hand, "but then I guess I'm lazy, and it is nice to be waited on."

Her mother poured herself a glass of tea and settled herself comfortably in her favorite chair across from Larcy. "Six days a week," she complained, "I've not one soul in this house to wait on, and here you are wanting to take the pleasure of my day away from me."

"Like fun I am," Larcy told her, grinning. She shook her head, "Whatever am I going to do when I get married and there's no one to wait on me except myself?"

Her mother took a swallow of tea, chewed slowly on a slice of orange. "When a woman is ready for marriage," she told Larcy, "she's ready to do the waiting on, not have it done for her."

Larcy delighted in teasing her mother. "Why, Mrs. Ryan," she said, "I do believe you think a man should be a woman's lord and master, the uncrowned king of the household, that it's his due to have his pipe and slippers brought to him at night, that. . . ."

Her mother set down the orange rind and took another swallow of tea. "There's nothing wrong in it," she told Larcy firmly, "the dear Lord made man the stronger, the wiser, so why shouldn't . . ."

Larcy shook her head and playfully got up and put a hand across her mother's lips. "Now, now," she said, "let's have no more of such sacrilegious talk. And . . . speaking of Pete, as we both know you were, has he gotten back from Ann Arbor?"

Her mother shook her head. "Margaret said he'd phoned he expected to be back around supper time, but with the weather the way it is, I wouldn't be surprised if he'd wait until morning."

Larcy felt a tug of disappointment. She said, "the taxi driver said the paper predicted a clearing by afternoon."

Her mother turned her head to look out of the window. "Wishful thinking," she said, "this isn't the kind of rain that pours and then is over. It's the kind that hangs on, sometimes for days.'"

"You," Larcy told her mother sadly, going back to her seat, "are exactly the kind of optimist I need."

Her mother said slowly, "Pete's growing up. You're looking at him and still seeing a boy, but he's no longer a boy, Larcy."

Larcy turned her eyes on her mother. "Are you trying to tell me something?"

Her mother gave her a smile and said, "Maybe I am."

It was a lovely, comfortable, wonderful day, and Larcy hated it to end. Contrary to the cab driver's predictions, the weather did not clear. If anything, the fog closed in tighter, and the rain fell more monotonously as if it had always rained, would always rain.

She closed her eyes and leaned back against the seat. The windows inside the bus were steamed over, it looked like night outside, but it was barely seven.

She'd had her mother's meat balls and spaghetti for lunch, and still felt uncomfortably full. Would

153

she ever be able to cook like her mother? She supposed not. It was probably one of the arts little girls used to be taught, for that great day when they'd take over the management of their own home.

She'd continue to work after she was married, somehow she'd have to make Pete see it was important to her, to be useful, helpful. She'd make him see.

And they'd spell each other on the cooking probably, or maybe even have a maid who'd stay all of the time, and do the cooking for them.

A little boy in the seat behind her squirmed and whispered, in a loud, carrying whisper that he had to go to the toilet. The mother said in an equally loud, carrying whisper, breaking at the edges with fatigue and impatience, that he'd just have to hold himself until they got home.

The child began to whine, in a low, unhappy voice. Larcy turned towards the window, rubbed a spot clear with one hand, and peered out of the uneven circle she'd made.

The way she was thinking lately, she thought, all Pete needed to do was to ask her again, and she'd say "yes." But would she? Would she?

Was it that absence made the heart grow fonder? But she'd been away from Pete before . . . those years at the university when she was in training . . . Pete's years at the university.

Or was it merely the very normalcy of Pete? Something sane and concrete to hold onto?

The spot she'd cleared had steamed over again. She closed her eyes, leaned back against the seat. She wasn't due until nine. When she got back, she'd go

upstairs, close the door to her room, and read. She hadn't had a chance to even look through the book she'd bought on Tuesday.

Thinking of Tuesday brought a picture of Bena sitting in the Coney Island talking so seriously with that awful, disreputable appearing young man.

Larcy frowned, opened her eyes, rubbed a spot clean again on the window, and stared out into the fog.

The rain had stopped by the time the bus reached her stop, but the fog was as damp and bone chilling as if it still rained. And it was not a pleasant walk this night, down the cut off that led from the highway to the house.

The gray fog was still and mysterious and occasionally as she ran, she'd tangle a foot in the roots of an old tree that had once stood where the cut off now was.

When she reached the house, running blindly, wildly as if footsteps followed behind her, she nearly stumbled into the car that was parked at the back door near the patio.

She went around to the front of the house, wiping at her hair that dripped rain, feeling the damp on the back of her neck, tasting it in her mouth.

The front hall was empty, but voices came from the long, low living room beyond. And Lyn's voice shouted, mocking and shrill, "Well, Larcy, guess what, Lieutenant Bricker says he knows who the murdered man is . . . was . . . past tense for dead, isn't it?"

Larcy walked slowly in from the hall. They were

all sitting there, Lyn, Bena, and the young Lieutenant not looking quite so young this time.

Bena looked up at Larcy from where she was sitting on the tan sofa, and said slowly, heavily, with an apologetic glance at the detective, "Lyn isn't quite so unfeeling as she tries to let on. The murdered man, Larcy, was my sister Marian's husband . . . Philip Francis."

Larcy thought, *I knew. Somehow, all of the time, I knew it was him.*

Chapter Sixteen

LIEUTENANT BRICKER said quietly, "Sit down, Miss Ryan."

"Yes, Larcy, *do* join the party," Lyn said. "We're playing a new game, it's called 'Murder, murder, who's got the murderer.' "

They all turned to stare at her, Bena frowning, Larcy dazed, the detective thoughtful.

Larcy advanced woodenly to the handiest chair which happened to be a straight back, hard seated one. She let herself down onto it slowly, holding her purse and gloves between her hands as if something horrible would happen if she dared let go of them.

Bena said, "You're back early, Larcy."

Larcy nodded. "The fog," she said, "I wanted to get back before it got worse."

The detective twisted around in his chair and looked directly at Larcy, his eyes probing her face, searching. She felt herself flush under that concentrated stare.

He said quietly, "You told me you'd seen lights from a car at Stalen Pier the night you were taking a walk, the night of the murder." His eyes seemed to comb her face. "Did you know then, Miss Ryan, who the murder victim was?"

"Of course I didn't know!" Larcy waxed indignant.

"I was too far away, I could see just this figure and the car lights . . . I told you . . ."

He said nothing for a moment and then said slowly, "But you did know this Philip Francis? You'd seen him before?"

Seen him before? Coldness pressed against Larcy's stomach. She didn't really know if she had seen him before. Bena had called that man *Phil,* but that didn't necessarily mean he was that Philip.

"Well, Miss Ryan," the detective said smoothly, "I'm waiting for your answer."

Slowly, carefully, Larcy shook her head. "No, lieutenant, I didn't know Philip Francis, and to my knowledge I've never seen him."

Her stomach unknotted a bit. It hadn't been a lie, she'd told the exact truth. To her knowledge she'd never seen him.

He said softly, quietly, "If you change your mind, Miss Ryan, you can tell me."

Why, Larcy thought, *why . . . he doesn't believe me! He thinks I know something about the murder. I'm sure he does.*

It was Bena's voice that cut into the sudden silence. She said, indignantly, "Why are you doing this to Larcy? Acting as if she's a criminal or something. She's worked for us less than a month. We never knew her until then. How would she know my brother-in-law? Marian and Philip lived in Chicago, not in Port Hope."

He tapped the fingers of his two hands together and said musingly, as if he'd heard not one word of

158

what Bena had said, "I presume you've very attached to your father. You're his only living relative?"

Bena nodded. "My mother died . . . twelve years ago, and my sister suffered a . . . nervous breakdown. She died a year ago last month."

He said smoothly, "You didn't answer my question completely, Mrs. Pierce."

Lyn said roughly, "I'll tell you for her, lieutenant, she hates him. She's only waiting for him to die so that she can get his money."

Bena's face crimsoned, something flashed in the smoky eyes, and then disappeared as if the look had never been there. She stared down at her clasped hands in the awful, shocked silence.

Larcy sat quietly in the hard chair, not daring to look at Bena.

The silence was pregnant with unvoiced sounds, and then Bena sighed and lifted her eyes to stare across the room at the detective.

"Lieutenant," she said, in the softest, saddest voice Larcy had ever heard, "my father is a very ill man," she angled a gaze for a moment, at Larcy who nodded, "he not only has a malignancy, but is a heart victim as well." Her sigh rippled again. "My father has always enjoyed making money, never spending it. The things most of us take for granted as necessities, are considered luxuries by my father." She stared around the room, dulled by the grayish fog that pressed in through the windows. "He . . . let my mother die because he considered it waste to pay for the specialist, the hospital . . . that might have saved her."

She shook her head, "No, lieutenant, I'm not attached to my father. I don't love him. He broke my heart too many times as a child, but . . . I don't wish him dead."

Larcy sat squelched and small in the hard chair, and for once Lyn merely watched, her eyes mocking and bright.

Feet moved on the floor making little crisps of sound. Lt. Bricker said slowly, his eyes veiled on Bena's face, "you say your father is practically a miser, and yet you have a maid, he has a nurse."

Bena said, "Sybil works for practically nothing. When I came here to take care of father, after my . . . husband went to sea . . . the deal was that Sybil was to come with me, or . . . I wouldn't come."

She looked at Larcy. "And as for his having a nurse," there was bitterness in her voice, "the doctor suggested it, and . . . father is willing to go to any lengths . . . to save his own life."

"And besides," Lyn said, her smile falsely sweet as she turned her gaze on Bena, "David's afraid of her. He's convinced she's 'out to do him in.'" She tossed her light hair, and then combed it by running the fingers of one hand through it.

"Oh, for heaven's sake, Aunt Bena . . . dear . . ." she tossed in scornfully, "don't look as if I've said something terribly shocking. It's true . . . he is afraid of you. Ask Larcy . . . he's said it in front of her."

He's going to ask me, Larcy thought, unhappily. And she'd have to tell him . . . Her hands toyed with the clasp of her purse, opening and closing it in a kind of monotonous rhythm.

160

When Lt. Bricker turning his probing eyes on her, she said, reluctantly, "When people are very ill, lieutenant, they . . . imagine things, quite often have hallucinations." She ran her tongue nervously over her dry lips. She was getting involved in it, and she did not wish to become involved at all.

"Mr. Magnam," she said slowly, unhappily, "doesn't trust . . . anyone. He . . . it's as if he constantly feels that someone . . . wants to kill him."

"I told you, didn't I?" Lyn said gleefully.

The detective asked, his voice Larcy knew, deceptively bland, "And you, Miss Ryan? Does he trust *you?*"

Larcy was forced to shake her head. "No," she said. "Not completely." She flung Bena an apologetic glance and said with unhappy desperation, "He . . . sometimes . . . seems to think that I was hired to . . ." the words caught in her throat.

Lyn said fiercely, "Go on and say it, Larcy, he thinks Bena hired you to kill him for her!"

Bena let out a soft, strangled moan. Larcy felt anger flare up in her. She said furiously to Lyn, forgetting everything but her anger, "you didn't have to say it like that . . . so brutally."

Lyn shrugged. "How can you say murder any way except brutally? Unless that is . . . you approve of murder. And you don't, do you, Larcy? You're so soft . . . so chicken."

Larcy felt heat stain her cheeks, her hands tightened around her purse and gloves. It wasn't fair, it was still her afternoon off, and instead of being up-

161

stairs reading as she'd planned, here she was, sitting in the dismal living room, being hounded, accused, blazed at . . .

She looked directly at Lyn and said, not even trying to stop the words from bursting forth, "He said . . . that you could stick a knife into a man . . . without blinking an eye."

Lyn merely gave that mocking grin and it so enraged Larcy for the moment that she blurted out, "You lied about giving him the newspaper. You did take it up to him. His door was closed, and you're the only one who does that, closes his door when he prefers it open."

She did think Lyn looked startled for a moment, but then Lyn shrugged and said, "All right, all right, I did take the paper up to him, but then I thought it over, and I decided it might not be a good thing, after all. He sees more things than he's given credit for seeing . . . I don't think he ever really sleeps in spite of all of that stuff Larcy keeps shooting into him . . . and he'd know right away it was Philip and he could get to thinking that Philip's murder could have something to do with him and . . ."

Lt. Bricker asked softly, "why would he think that?"

Lyn shook her head impatiently, "How would I know? You're the detective."

He turned his gaze sharply on Bena, "Why do you think he'd think that, Mrs. Pierce?"

Bena shook her head, "Perhaps," she suggested, "because of his overworked imagination? Larcy said that people as ill as father . . ." she looked con-

162

fused suddenly, as if she wished she had not started this line of reasoning. She bit at her under lip, frowned unhappily at the detective. "Father collects . . . macabre newspaper clippings," she said, "pastes them in his scrapbook. He could have thought with Marian dead and then Philip, that perhaps he'd be next, a kind of violent thread going through the entire family . . ."

Lyn said, "I read a novel like that once, where everybody was killed and there was no motive for the murders. But there is a motive here, isn't there, lieutenant?" She frowned suddenly and flashed her gaze on Larcy. She said, "I want to finish what I was telling you. After I'd gone to bed I got to thinking about it and I thought maybe I'd go and get the newspaper. I didn't want to be part of anything that might happen to David. Not that I have any love for him, but I just didn't want to get myself involved. So . . . I slipped into his bedroom and got the paper and took it outside in the fireplace and burned it."

Larcy caught her breath sharply as a thought exploded in her mind. What if David had lied about not having seen the newspaper? What if he'd already read about the murder before Lyn had taken the paper? What if . . .

"You've thought of something." The detective's voice slithered its way into her consciousness.

"Thought of something?" Larcy stared dazedly at him, blinked her eyes, licked her dry, tasteless lips. "I don't know," she said, frowning, reluctant, "I just thought . . ." she gave Bena an unhappy glance, "what if Mr. Magnam *had* read the newspaper account of the murder before . . . Lyn took away the newspaper And what if he . . . was afraid and . . . and wasn't asleep when Lyn came into the bedroom. She said it was after everybody had already gone to bed, and . . . it's dark in the hall and there's only the night light burning in his room . . . he wouldn't have been able to see her clearly . . ."

"And thought she was someone who had come to harm him? Is that what you're meaning, Miss Ryan?" the detective's voice broke crisply into her words.

Larcy nodded miserably. She said, "Tuesday night Mr. Magnam had a very bad spell. The doctor said it was caused by over excitement, only there wasn't any excitement, nothing at all unusual . . . except the murder, and if he'd read the newspaper and got frightened and lay there in the darkness tense and . . . and ready to try and defend himself against someone, it could have caused the . . . attack."

Lyn's voice was high and shrill, "You're saying that it was me who caused him to . . ." She shook her head, shrugged, sighed. "And after I did try to be so decent about it."

Lt. Bricker turned his hard, blue gaze on her. He said softly, "Mr. Magnam knew who the murder victim was. How did you know he knew this?"

"Simple," Lyn said, in her mocking, jarring voice, "because Philip was here. He was upstairs to talk to David. I saw him there, heard them."

Larcy saw that Bena's face went a ghastly white at Lyn's words. "That isn't true," she jerked out. "He wouldn't go to father. I told him . . ."

164

She turned slowly, fearfully towards the detective, as if suddenly conscious of what she had said. "All right," she said, in a soft, low voice that spelled defeat, "I saw Philip, talked to him. I . . . asked him to let me handle it, not to go to father."

Lyn laughed. "And you think Philip would listen to you? He'd go where he wanted to go, he'd laugh at you."

"You say you saw Philip Francis, talked to him," the detective persisted. "When was this, Mrs. Pierce?"

"When?" Bena stared at him, seemingly dazed. "Oh, when? Monday afternoon. He'd phoned me the night before, insisted on coming to the house . . . I thought I'd talked him out of it . . . I told him I'd meet him on the beach, that we'd talk." She shook her head unhappily. "I didn't kill him, lieutenant."

The detective allowed a brief smile to hover about his lips for a second. "You haven't been accused of murder, Mrs. Pierce." He leaned forward towards her. "You say you talked to him . . . what did you talk about?"

Bena said, her hands shaking but her voice holding a certain calmness, "I don't think that's pertinent to your case, lieutenant. He was my brother-in-law . . . had been my brother-in-law . . . we had things in common to talk about."

"Important enough," he told her softly, "that you didn't want him coming to the house, that he phoned you in the middle of the night insisting on seeing you?"

Lyn said, "he wanted money. He always wanted

165

money. He had something on Bena, or Johnson, or both of them. I'm sure of it."

"Johnson?" Lieutenant Bricker's thick, light brows shot upwards.

Lyn said impatiently, "Bena's husband. He had to have something . . . why else would he demand money from Bena? I don't mean ask for it . . . demand it, as if he knew he would get it." She flashed Bena a sly look. "He said . . . I heard him say it . . . to David that afternoon . . . 'I'll get the money, one way or another.' And David laughed and told him he wasn't getting any money from him, one way or another, he'd see him dead first."

Lt. Bricker turned to look at Bena and said softly, "And now he is dead, isn't he, Mrs. Pierce?" He flashed the question at her with the rapidity of a gun firing. "Why didn't you tell me you knew who the victim was, the first time I called here? You'd have saved the police a bit of work. Didn't you know we'd find out who he was? And then wonder why it was that you hadn't told us?"

Bena shook her head frantically. "I didn't know at first, lieutenant. I didn't know."

"But you had suspicions, didn't you?" he persisted.

Bena said slowly, "If people ran to the police every time they held a suspicion of someone. . . ."

He said gently, "You're evading the issue, Mrs. Pierce. The fact of it is that you knew and did not tell the police." His blue eyes darkened and steel came into his voice. "What hold did Philip Francis have on you or your husband?"

Bena shook her head. "No hold, lieutenant. He

166

came to me for money, yes, he . . . Phil was never a man for holding on to a job, and he'd just gotten out of jail. I . . . wanted to help him, if I could. After all he was my sister's husband."

Lt. Bricker smiled at her, got carefully to his feet. He looked at Bena, at Lyn, at Larcy, shook his head. He said pleasantly, "I'm a very careful, diligent man. I collect scraps, I discard nothing. I'm like a bull dog, or is it an elephant . . . but in the end, I want to warn you, I usually come up with the person, or persons, responsible for a crime."

Nobody in the room seemed able to move as the detective walked out of the living room into the hall, and then Bena as if conscious suddenly, of her manners, got stiffly to her feet.

"I'll see you to the door, lieutenant."

Lyn looked at Larcy and laughed, "That's auntie," she said, "always wanting to do the proper thing at the proper moment, but she never does. Such a fraud she is."

Chapter Seventeen

SATURDAY MORNING Pete phoned. Larcy found herself inordinately glad to hear from him. She clung to the phone and talked too fast, in jerky, disconnected sentences.

"Whoa," he said, "whoa, you're talking a mile a minute, Larcy, and I can't make out half of what you're saying." She heard the sudden anxiety in his voice, "Is something wrong?"

"Wrong?" Larcy's voice lifted the single word, left it poised in the air for a second. "Of course not. It's just that I'm so glad to hear your voice. Do you know I haven't seen you in over a week?"

Her hands were tight against the phone. That wasn't what she wanted to say, what she wanted to say was, "I want you to come out here. Pete, I want to talk to you, there are certain . . . things. I'm frightened."

But Sybil was standing behind her in the hall, armed with the vacuum cleaner and its attachments. Deliberately? Had Sybil deliberately come into the hall, knowing Larcy was at the telephone?

Pete was saying, "It's nice to hear you say that, but I don't believe a word of it." The anxiety sounded stronger in his voice. "You don't sound like yourself. I'm coming out there, Larcy."

"Sunday?" Larcy raised her voice as if he'd asked a question. "Why yes, I'm usually free from three until five. Bring your bathing suit, and we'll have a swim. I can hardly wait to see you."

She hung up quickly in the midst of Pete's explosive, "Sunday! Larcy, I don't understand any of this, I . . ."

Larcy turned slowly from the phone, and widened her eyes on seeing Sybil, as if she hadn't known she was there. "Oh, Sybil," she said, "I'm sorry, am I holding you up?"

The dark, gaunt woman shook her head, said coldly, "If I'd figured on vacuuming in here, I'd have gone ahead and done it. I'm going to do the living room, strangers traipsing in and out all of the time, tracking in sand . . ."

Larcy watched her move into the other room. To offer to help her carry the attachments would be useless, because her offer would be rudely refused.

She sighed and went on upstairs. She was frowning as she walked along the hall, with the sunshine making a path like a rug runner unevenly down the middle of the boards.

She should have controlled herself better with Pete. She'd left him anxious, worried about her, and a worried Pete . . . her frown deepened, and then she shook her head, no Pete wouldn't rush into something. Pete was cautious, after all, he was training to be a lawyer. He'd worry, but he'd wait, come out tomorrow afternoon as she'd told him.

She sighed and felt a tiny disappointment. Was it that she wanted him to be impulsive? Rushing about, not knowing where he was going, or why?

Was Johnson Pierce like that? Dashing, impulsive,

169

unthinking, uncaring? Pete wasn't uncaring. Pete was the caring kind, the enduring kind. A sudden rush of tenderness shook her. She did not want Pete to change. It suddenly occurred to her. She wanted Pete to be Pete . . . as she wanted her mother to remain her mother, corny, cheerful, filled to the brim with all of the old idioms . . .

She stopped in the doorway of David Magnam's room, and watched him, feeling a sense almost of panic.

He had pulled himself . . . with what grim, determined effort, she could only imagine . . . high up on the pillow, and was jerking his right arm back and forth in a kind of stabbing motion.

Stabbing motion! Terror slid down her arms, trembled in the tips of her fingers. That was exactly what he was doing, using the scissors he was holding in his right hand as if it was a weapon . . . a knife.

His voice thundered at her weakly, "Shocks you, don't it?" Impatiently, "Well, come on around in front so's I can see you. Don't stand there shaking your head behind my back."

Larcy walked around in front of the bed. He seemed always to know when she came into the room, without turning his head, without looking at her.

It was almost as if he knew by the way a person's footsteps sounded on the rug . . . the way they breathed.

If that was true, then why hadn't he known it was Lyn when she'd come into the room? Or . . . had he known it was Lyn?

The terrible significance of such thinking shook

170

her. She brushed aside the thought. Lyn was young, mocking, hurt, bitter, but she was not likely to commit murder. People who did murder, usually did not talk about it. Everyone knew that. Didn't they?

She forced her voice to a steadiness she was far from feeling. "No," she told David Magnam, shaking her head, "I'm not shocked, but I don't think Dr. Ule would approve of you using your arms the way you were doing. It's rather violent exercise for a man who spends all of his time lying in bed."

He glared at her. "To hell with Ule." But he did put away the scissors.

A frown cut across Larcy's face, and a certainty knotted her stomach. She said, looking directly at David Magnam, so that she could see his face, "Mr. Magnam, you weren't exercising your arms like that Tuesday night, were you?"

His face didn't change expression. He said, with a look of contempt, "You'd like to know what I do and don't do, the times you aren't in here, wouldn't you, Miss Bedpan?" He tossed the name off with relish, his eyes glinting on her face.

Larcy shook her head and said quietly, "Mr. Magnam, the only reason I asked, was that, if you were, then you'd better stop that kind of exertion. Or don't you remember what happened Tuesday night?"

"I was supposed to die," he told her gleefully, "but I didn't die, did I?"

Larcy said gently, "You have to obey doctor's orders, Mr. Magnam."

He frowned up at her, his eyes baleful, and then he said slowly, as if he was enjoying it, "I told you

171

I knew who was murdered. He had to be killed, you know." His eyes swung past Larcy's face, and although he couldn't see the doorway, he raised his voice and said, "Come on in, Bena. We both know Philip had to be killed."

There was a pause and Bena's voice said from the doorway, "No, I'm not coming in." There was a touch of . . . anxiety? . . . in her voice. "Why do you think I . . . thought Philip . . . should be killed?"

He said, a mocking sarcasm in his voice, reminding Larcy of Lyn. "I don't spit all my seeds out in one spot, I save some of them for another spot, another time." His voice softened, he said, almost in a whisper, "I got the murderer figured out, too."

Bena's voice came quietly, "If you know that, father, you should tell it to that detective who came here. I'll phone him . . ."

David Magnam's voice was cloudy with irritation. He said, "When I'm ready to talk, I'll talk. You keep him away from me."

Bena's sigh cut gently into the room. She said, "I think I'll lie down, Larcy. If anything comes up and you need me, call me."

David Magnam said, his voice menacing, ugly, "What she means is, if I look like I'm ready to die, she wants to be on hand to see it happen."

There was no answer to that, and Larcy made none. She heard the quick, sharp, tap of Bena's heels on the bare boards as she continued on down the hall.

Larcy walked over to the large window and stared

out at the wealth of sand, of blue green water. Was David Magnam telling the truth? Did he know who the murderer was?

And if he did know, was his life in danger? She brushed one hand restlessly across one side of her face. Down at the lake gulls flew back and forth over the water, darting downwards as they spied some morsel on the sand or water, that attracted them.

There was such a haunting loneliness, such eerie sadness in their cries that it invariably brought the shivers to Larcy.

She turned slowly from the window, one hand sliding down the side of the curtains, as if loath to let go. Of course his life would be in danger if he actually knew who had killed Philip Francis, and if the murderer knew that he knew . . .

And there was the catch. Did the murderer know? Did David Magnam truly know? Or had he merely said what he had, in order to frighten Bena?

Larcy thought unhappily, *here I am, off again. Why would he want to frighten Mrs. Pierce? Because he thought she had done the killing?*

Or . . . because Bena knew who had done the killing, and that person was very important to her? So important that she would stop at nothing in order to keep David Magnam from repeating to the wrong ears the name of the murderer?

Icy fingers moved relentlessly up Larcy's spine. That could mean only one person . . . Bena's husband, Johnson Pierce!

Sound seemed to be locked tightly in Larcy's throat, locked so tightly that it seemed as if that sound would explode, wildly, fiercely, when her throat became unlocked. So that she had to move her muscles slowly, carefully, so that the explosion would not happen. The tips of her fingers were cold, the palms of her hands warm and wet.

Johnson Pierce was in the navy. His ship was out at sea. Didn't Bena receive almost daily letters from him?

Still . . . how do I know he's at sea? Larcy asked herself relentlessly. *Because Mrs. Pierce tells me this?*

He could be any place, in any city. She wet her dry lips with the tip of a nervous tongue. He could be right in Port Hope.

She became aware of David Magnam's fierce gaze. He said, his lips curling in what, for him, passed as a smile, "Scared her, didn't I?" he gloated. "Let her think about it for a while. Do her good."

He didn't know. There was a feeling of relief in Larcy. A frown wrinkled the smooth, tanned skin of her forehead. If David Magnam did know, he would say nothing, he'd hold his information over that person's head, strangling with it, shriveling . . .

The tang of the lake blew in the open window. David Magnam said crossly, "Horrible smell. Close that window. No, dammit, leave it open, it gets too hot when it's closed."

Larcy walked slowly down the uncarpeted stairs. Sunlight lay like a warm brightness on the floor, dappled the walls, sparkled across the pictured eyes of Johnson Pierce.

A house of warmth, sunshine, love. Larcy's eyes darkened, and fear shadowed her face, lay heavy against her heart. It was a house of clouds and fog, of ugliness, of suspicion and . . . hate.

She hunched her shoulders forward, feeling coldness press against her chest.

Bena Pierce had received a letter only yesterday from her husband. Hadn't Larcy seen it in her hand? But what had she seen, Larcy wondered unhappily, only an envelope, only the address: *Mrs. Johnson Pierce, Lakeside, Michigan, USA.*

Her spirits lifted as it came to her——*USA*—— that had to mean the letter had been sent from a foreign port.

Lyn twisted around to face Larcy when Larcy walked into the dining room. She looked irritable and cross, "I wish I didn't have to look at such a silly, ridiculous happy face," she stormed. "You do look as if someone had left you a hundred million dollars."

The brown eyes widened. She said lightly, "Oh, my, David didn't tell you he was going to remake his will and leave his whole fortune to you, did he?"

Larcy merely laughed. It was senseless to try and talk to Lyn when she was in the ugly mood she was in now.

Larcy walked through the dining room and out onto the patio. The tops of the scrub pines were touched with sunshine, the dark spaces between the trees did not look so dark or so shadowed.

Larcy let her gaze dwell on them idly as she frowned in concentrated thought. "Lyn?" Was Lyn important enough to Bena that Bena would . . .

Larcy shook her head. It didn't make sense. *Bena,*

then? She stared miserably down at her hands. She was no detective. She was a nurse. What was she trying to do, for heaven's sake? Play detective?

David Magnam had lied about knowing who the killer was. She was sure he'd lied. David Magnum was a man confined to his room, to his bed, needing the services of a private nurse. How then, did she expect that he would know about something like a murder that had happened someplace else?

Larcy saw a movement near the kitchen door. Her stomach tensed and her knees drew together. The rat Sybil had said she was still trying to catch? Larcy had almost forgotten about the rat.

She moved now, carefully, cautiously past the garbage cans, the trash barrel. Inside the kitchen Sybil was ironing. As Larcy came in the door, she put up a hand and wiped the back of it across her forehead.

"Hot," she said, deigning to recognize the fact that Larcy stood in the doorway.

Larcy said, "I saw another rat. Just now." She waved a hand. "Out there."

"Oh?" Sybil turned the flat, dull eyes towards the door. "Likely the same one you saw last time," she said. "Rats are hard to catch. Traps or poison, it don't make much difference." She shook her head, ran the iron along the collar of a blouse. "Not that I'm going to try poison again. I don't like having it around. That rat gets caught, it'll be by trapping."

Her lips set, thinned, "Poison's cruel," she said, "a horrible way to die. I don't like it." Her words were jerky, cut short, as if being snipped off, one by one by a pair of scissors.

Scissors! Larcy's stomach lurched as she remembered the scene she'd walked onto in David Magnam's room, of David propped up against the pillows using the scissors with that jerky, stabbing motion, as if he were using them . . . against someone.

Sybil seemed to think her sudden shiver concerned the rat she'd seen. "Rats don't attack humans," she said, "no matter what stories some people tell you." She gave a sharp, thin laugh, "Besides, our rats are very well fed."

Larcy thought curiously as she walked out of the kitchen, that it was the first time she'd heard Sybil laugh.

Pete showed up exactly at three. Larcy seeing his car hurried out to meet him, but Bena was there first. When Larcy reached Pete, Bena was extending her hand, saying in her soft, sad, warm voice, "You're Pete." Shaking her dark head at him, "of course you are. Larcy has never described you, but I knew you would look like this."

Pete smiled, said something in a low voice which Larcy couldn't hear, and looked past Bena at Larcy.

"Hi," he said, in a loud, carrying voice, "long time no see."

"Long time no see," Larcy flung back, feeling suddenly comforted, feeling that she wished Bena would go away, let her and Pete alone.

"Pete," Larcy said, walking over to stand beside him. "This is Mrs. Pierce."

Bena smiled at her gently. She said, "He's very sweet, Larcy. Exactly the way I had pictured him to be."

An odd feeling of resentment touched Larcy. What right did Bena have in trying to picture Pete, anyway? Before she was able to laugh herself out of that, Lyn appeared.

Lyn in blue shorts and a white blouse, her long legs very tanned, very slender, her brown eyes smudgy, her mouth red and mocking.

She put both hands on her slender hips and cocked her head flirtatiously at Pete. "Of course you're the way Aunt Bena pictured you, blond and clean cut, the All-American ideal of manhood. How else would you look, being Larcy's boy friend?"

Larcy saw the look of astonishment light Pete's face. "Well," he said, "I don't know whether to accept that as a compliment or not."

Lyn lowered her lids so that her thick lashes nearly obscured her eyes. She said, "I think everyone should make their own decisions." She allowed her eyes to open wide and asked, "Do I look the way you had pictured me?"

Pete was not always the most tactful man in the world, as Larcy had discovered on numerous occasions. He said lightly, "I don't know how I had pictured you. Larcy never got around to talking about you."

Larcy saw a dark flush stain Lyn's cheeks, but then she shrugged, laughed lightly and said, with a glance at Larcy, "Knowing Larcy, I should have expected she wouldn't."

Bena smiled at Larcy, managed to look helpless and unhappy. She swung her gaze to Pete, and said, with a gesture towards Lyn, "this is Lyn Francis, who lives here with my father and me. She's very young and . . ." she flung a smile at Lyn, a smile that did not touch her eyes . . . "brash, as the very young so often are."

"My . . . my . . . my," Lyn said, "aren't we maternal and understanding?" She whirled around and flew back to the house.

Larcy looked at Pete. "Did you bring your bathing suit?"

"Naturally." Pete gave her a warm grin, "don't I usually do what I'm told?"

Bena gave a polite laugh, told Pete he could change in the house. And walked ahead, leaving Pete and Larcy to walk together.

It was the only time in two hours Pete was there that he and Larcy had any time to be alone.

They walked down to the beach together, and Pete asked in a low voice, "Why did you act so closed up . . . so funny, the other night when you phoned?"

Larcy shook her head. "It's a long story," she told him. "Let's have a swim first, and then we'll lie on the beach and talk."

But before they came out of the water, Lyn appeared in her bathing suit, and swam with them.

And then, when they came out of the water Bena sauntered down carrying a picnic basket and a thermos of lemonade.

When it was time for Pete to leave, Larcy frowned

179

up at him and said wryly, "we didn't have any time in which to talk."

Pete said, "She was only trying to be polite."

Larcy's frown deepened. Had there been impatience in Pete's voice?

She watched the car disappear down the gravel of the cutoff that led to the highway. Had Bena been only polite? Or . . . was there a deeper meaning in the fact that she had not left Larcy alone with Pete for over five minutes at a time?

Because she was afraid of what Larcy might tell Pete? The raucous cry of a crow screamed across the sky, she could hear the sound of Pete's car braking as it hit the turn onto the highway.

She had the most awful feeling of having had her fears pushed aside, dismissed . . . impatiently.

Bena's voice sounded directly behind her. "You must have him come again, Larcy, he's a fine boy." And then, in a softer, almost apologetic voice, "Father's awake and he wants you." She spread her hands, "you know father when he begins wanting somebody."

Larcy smiled at her, turned around and walked inside the house and up the stairs to David Magnam's room.

He had turned on his transistor radio, and the slightly nasal voice of the news broadcaster said, "this reporter has been told by reliable sources that the police have a definite lead on the killer of Philip Francis whose body was found Monday night in a rowboat just off Stalen Pier."

Chapter Eighteen

LARCY stood still, listening, a feeling of relief flowing over her. She wanted it to be over, done with. It was the closest she'd ever come to murder, and she wanted to put it in the far back part of her mind and never bring it out again.

That young Lieutenant Bricker had said he always kept plugging away until he found the person or persons responsible for a crime. And she'd thought, hadn't she, that he'd meant someone in this house. But she'd been wrong.

The breeze blew in from the lake, bringing a clean, fresh smell. She permitted herself a deep, slow breath of intense relief. Now the murderer would be arrested, arraigned (wasn't that what it was called?) and the tenseness, the fear, would be gone.

A feeling of dismay hit her. The fear, the tenseness had been there long before the murder had happened. Why then would she suppose it would be gone with the arrest of the murderer?

There was a click as David Magnam switched off the radio. There was a malevolent gleam in his eyes. "You'd like him to be caught, wouldn't you, Larcy?" he flung at her. "You think then you could lie easy in your bed." He gave that sharp, barking laugh of his. "People are always demanding the police catch the murderer, the robber, the kidnapper. The police have to throw out little hints that they're just about ready to pop down on the criminal. That way the people are satisfied."

He gave a scornful snort. "The murderer isn't about to be caught. Let's say I know this."

A shiver of fear ran over Larcy, but she managed to keep it under control. She said lightly, treating it as a joke, "you can't possibly know that, Mr. Magnam." She set the radio on the table by the bed. "You read too much about crime and criminals."

"You'd like to think that, wouldn't you?" he told her.

He seemed not to want to continue the discussion, but closed his eyes. Larcy moved about the room straightening, smoothing. Bena had said he'd wanted her, but whatever it was he'd wanted, so far he'd not mentioned it.

Had he wanted her to hear the broadcast? She shrugged, felt unhappy, wished Pete hadn't gone off impatient with her, wished it was Thursday, wished . . .

His voice startled her. "Who was the man here today?"

She turned around to look at him. He lay upstairs here, cut off from the downstairs, and yet he seemed to know more of what was going on than did those who were involved. It frightened her. "A friend of mine," she told him, "Pete Crimmins . . . Mrs. Pierce said it was all right for me to have him come out anytime."

His eyes narrowed on her face, he said, "and Bena kept you both company, and if it wasn't Bena, it was Lyn."

Larcy stared at him, and her face went warm. She said carefully, "Both Mrs. Pierce and Lyn were very friendly. I appreciated it. So did Pete."

He shook his head, closed his eyes again, said, "You're a fool."

Larcy thought, "I have no right resenting him saying it, when I've been thinking the same thing myself."

Who did he think had killed Philip Francis? And was he right about the police not knowing? She wished she had not let her thoughts run along that line. It sent cold shivers sparkling up and down her legs, along the base of her spine.

She turned her gaze on the window. "It's a lovely day," she told him. "The water temperature came up to 63 today."

A snort was the only indication he gave that he'd heard her.

At six she brought him his supper, stayed until he'd eaten, then went downstairs and had her own, chicken salad, a cucumber sandwich and a gelatin salad.

Bena was in a non-talkative mood. She gave Larcy a vague smile when she came into the dining room, then concentrated on nibbling at her salad and staring out of the window.

Lyn did not show up for supper at all. And after she had eaten, Bena disappeared someplace. Sybil slammed and banged things in the kitchen, as an indication of her mood.

Larcy, feeling the depressive gloom of the house close about her, in spite of the bright, cheery late afternoon, went upstairs, got out the book she'd bought, lay across her bed, and tried to find interest in the witty, sparkling protagonists in the book, and did not find them either witty or sparkling, but unbearably dull.

At eight-thirty she took care of David Magnam's medicine. Before she left his room, she heard Lyn come up the stairs.

It was always easy to tell Lyn. She rarely walked, she ran, digging her heels hard and defiantly into the stairs. And then she would always slam the door of her room fiercely behind her.

"She thinks she knows," he said. "She don't know a half of it." There was a speculative look in his eyes.

Was he talking of Lyn? Larcy wondered. Lyn who didn't know the half of what?

She shook her head. She was not going to pursue the subject. She permitted herself a faint sigh. The thing to do was to keep yourself from thinking, speculating.

There was nothing in Monday's newspaper to indicate that the police had taken the murderer into custody.

David Magnam laughed when she took the newspaper up to him. He said smugly, "told you they didn't know anything, didn't I?"

Larcy felt that ball of fear wind and unwind inside of her. Did David know what he was talking about? Did he truly know who the murderer was? And was it . . . someone in the house . . . as he slyly hinted?

184

She dismissed the thought, refused to allow her mind to dwell on it. She was not a character in a murder melodrama. She was a person who had always been blessed . . . or cursed . . . with too vivid an imagination.

She forced herself into a cheerful sense of security she was far from feeling. And when she encountered Lyn in the hall downstairs later, it was as if Lyn too, was on her best behavior.

She asked Larcy if she'd mind keeping her company for a swim when she was free.

Larcy, overcome with astonishment, managed to hide it. Lyn did not ask, Lyn demanded, and became impatient if she could not have what she wanted, at the very moment of her demand.

"I'd like that," she told Lyn.

It was an hour before she was free. She put on her bathing suit, flung on her beach robe, remembering, reluctantly, the time she'd gone without it, and been forced to walk back along the highway.

She pushed the remembrance out of her mind. She was not going to think of that time, or any of the other times that had nothing, really, to do with her.

It was a lovely, wonderful afternoon, the water was warmer than it had been all summer. She was going to enjoy a swim and then later lie on the sand and add to her tan.

Still, she wasn't sure but that Lyn wouldn't have already changed her mind and gone swimming without her, or given up the idea entirely.

She was faintly surprised to see Lyn, in her bathing suit, a towel hanging from her shoulders, standing at the door looking out over the lake.

She turned around, and said, as if she knew what had been on Larcy's mind, "Surprised you, didn't I?"

Larcy flushed, and acknowledged with a wry grimace that Lyn had, certainly surprised her.

"Ready?" Lyn said, and without waiting for Larcy's answer flew out of the screen door and down the three steps to the sandy rise that led to the beach.

By the time Larcy reached the water Lyn was already wading out into the deeper part.

Larcy spread her towel, set down her bottle of sun tan lotion, and took off her beach robe. Lyn was floating lazily when Larcy reached her.

Larcy shivered as she immersed her body. Unlike the smaller inland lakes, the great lakes always seemed cold. She shook the hair back off her face . . . she detested bathing caps . . . and swam easily, invigorated by the coldness of the water.

After a few minutes, Lyn said gaily, "Race you. We'll each swim as far out as we can, and the one who swims the farthest is the winner."

Larcy shook her head, her eyes gazing out across the blue-green water that seemed unending. "I'm not a very good swimmer, I've never tried to swim very far."

Lyn laughed at her, suddenly mocking. "Oh, Larcy, if you're always going to be too scaredy cat to try anything . . ." Her eyes moved past Larcy and off to the side where the brown-green outlines of a small island showed in the distance. "Why," she said calmly, "I wouldn't be scared to swim clear to Simms Island, and that's four miles away."

Larcy shook her head, laughed, "You'd never make it."

Lyn said delightedly, "Want to bet?"

"No," Larcy said. She laughed again. "I do believe you'd try it on a bet." They weren't idle words. She felt a certainty that Lyn would try just that.

She swam out to a place in the water where she could stand up. Lyn followed her and Larcy asked, jerking her head towards the island. "Does anyone live there?"

Lyn shook her wet hair back from her face. "Live there!" she shuddered. "Who'd want to? There's a tiny beach . . . we took the boat over a few times, but mostly it's marshy." She made a face. "I don't know if there are any snakes on the island, but I'm not one for finding out. A place like that makes me think of snakes slithering around. And when it comes to snakes, I'm as chicken as you, Larcy."

Larcy said, turning her eyes reluctantly away from the island, "I don't like snakes, but I'm not actually afraid of them."

Lyn's eyes widened. She said, "You surprise me, Larcy, you really do. How about that race?"

"No," Larcy said, "I don't think so. You'd win. As soon as I begin realizing the water is way over my head I begin to panic. It wouldn't be a race at all."

Lyn said petulantly, "All right, I'll swim out by myself and see how far out I can go before I have to turn back."

Larcy said, "If you tire yourself out swimming as far out as you can, you won't have any energy left for the swim back."

Lyn just laughed. "If I start to drown," she said, "you will come out after me, won't you, Larcy? And you do know artificial respiration, so you see, there's really nothing for me to worry about."

Larcy, shading her eyes from the glare of the sun, watched Lyn swim out and out, until she was merely a dot on the wide surface of the lake.

When she was becoming panicky, Lyn reversed her course and began the backwards swim. When she reached Larcy, she stood up, breathing in deep gasps. She stripped the water from her hair by running both hands down the sides. Her eyelashes were glued together, and the thick part of her eyebrows stood up like tiny wings.

She gave a breathless laugh and said mockingly, "I told you, didn't I, that I could swim clear to Simms Island if I ever took the notion."

Sometimes swimming, sometimes wading, she moved out of the lake onto the beach. She was lying stomach down on the sand when Larcy came out to throw herself down on her towel and begin rubbing herself dry. She glanced over at Lyn and said mildly, "You're getting all sandy."

Lyn shrugged without bothering to turn over. "Most of it will brush off after I'm dry," she said.

Larcy began spreading herself with the sun tan oil. Lyn watched her for a second and then reached for the bottle. "I always forget to bring mine," she said.

"One of these days I'm going to look at myself and see a sun-dried, shriveled up old wreck."

She undid the straps of her swimming suit and began lathering herself generously with Larcy's oil.

When she'd finished she threw the bottle back at Larcy. Larcy said, feeling for the first time, as if Lyn were any young girl, "You look like a roast of meat all ready for the barbecue pit."

Lyn's giggle sounded young and girlish. "I don't think it's exactly a compliment." And then the giggle passed and the old mocking sound was back again in Lyn's voice.

She said, "What were you afraid of, Larcy? That I'd urge you to go too far out and then swim away and leave you?"

Larcy flushed. Why did Lyn have to spoil it? She said slowly, "Why would I think a thing like that? It would be very silly."

Lyn rolled over onto her back, and then into a sitting position. She leaned towards Larcy. "Don't be too sure," she told her, "it could just have been on my mind. I'm really not very stable . . . you really should know that."

"Nonsense," Larcy said, denying the hard knot that pressed against the pit of her stomach. She frowned and said, against her will, "why do you have to always say such silly things? Why can't you be . . ."

Lyn, jumping to her feet, took the word from Larcy. "Nice?" she said. She whirled around, bent down to pick up the towel she hadn't used. "Because my dear,

189

stupid Larcy, I am not nice. I'd hate to be nice. It has such an . . . an antiseptic sound to it."

She dashed up the hill towards the house, as if bored with Larcy, bored with the beach.

Larcy sighed, stayed perhaps another twenty minutes, and then left the beach. She walked slowly, thoughtfully. She had been afraid. Afraid to swim out too far? Or . . . afraid of Lyn?

Nonsense, she told herself, nonsense. The lake was full of swimmers, well, there were swimmers, and they weren't too far down the beach. She'd had only to call out for help. She would not have drowned.

She was frowning as she walked inside the house. She was forever allowing Lyn to get under her skin. And that, after all, was Lyn's prime purpose.

She stood that night at her window staring out towards Simms Island, dark and forlorn and brooding so far out in the lake. It was funny, wasn't it, that with all of the people wanting their own private island, no one had thought to buy Simms Island?

But then, who would want an island that consisted, as Lyn, at least, had told her, of only a tiny beach and miles of marshland?

On Tuesday Bena asked if Larcy would mind taking Wednesday off instead of Thursday.

"I hate to ask you, Larcy," Bena said, in her warmest, softest, saddest voice, "but something has come up and I have to be gone Thursday afternoon."

Larcy said, "It doesn't matter to me, Mrs. Pierce." She'd have to phone Pete, let him know she'd be in tomorrow instead of on Thursday. And her mother.

She smiled at Bena Pierce. She said, "My mother will be happy to see me a day early."

Bena's carefully arched brows raised. "And Pete?" she said. "Won't he be delighted, too, Larcy?"

Larcy was not going to let herself become involved in a discussion of her feelings toward Pete and his toward her. She grinned, shook her head, said philosophically, "One never knows about Pete."

Bena said slowly, "I'd say it differently, Larcy. One, I think, would always know about Pete. He appeared to me to be the reliable, dependable type of man." One hand reached out and touched Larcy's shoulder. "The kind the very best husbands are made from," she said.

Later Larcy thought that Bena had sounded almost . . . condescending, as if reliability and dependability were very commendable virtues, but very dull ones.

Larcy felt a flash of loyalty toward Pete. He was not at all dull. Well . . . most times he wasn't.

She tried unsuccessfully to get Pete and when there still wasn't any answer at 10:30 p.m. she gave up. She'd phone him in the morning before leaving, she decided.

She had to phone twice before she caught her mother at home. "It seems to me," she told her, "you could stay home at least some of the time."

"Larcy?" her mother said, "Larcy, is that you?" The quick anxiety in her voice. "Is something wrong?"

"I don't know," Larcy told her. "I'm coming home tomorrow instead of Thursday. But if you don't want me," she couldn't resist saying teasingly.

"The idea," her mother spluttered. "Such talk. I didn't bring you up to be flippant, my girl."

They talked for a few minutes and Larcy asked about Pete. "I've tried and tried to phone him," she said, "and nobody answers."

Her mother said, "Pete's been working someplace every evening this past week, so he's probably at work and Margaret's either out, or gone to bed. Do you know it's after ten-thirty?"

Larcy laughed and said, "Why mother, I know sometimes when you've stayed up as late as ten forty-five."

On that happy note, Larcy hung up. David Magnam's door was pulled almost shut when she passed it. She stopped, frowned, opened the door farther, leaned over David to make certain he was all right before going on to her own room.

The door wasn't closed, she could have forgotten and closed it that far herself. *But I didn't,* she thought, *I never do.*

Lyn's voice sounded out of the shadows. She said, "Larcy, you're scared again, and all because dear David's door was closed more than when you left it." She sighed. "Dear, dear," she said, "I shall have to be more careful when I look in on him. I thought certainly that I'd left the door exactly as I'd found it. You'd make a detective, Larcy. Why don't you apply for a job with that handsome, terribly brutal Lieutenant Bricker?"

Larcy said, "Mr. Magnam gets terribly upset if his door is closed."

192

Lyn said lightly, "It's either fear or claustrophobia. Which do you think it is, Larcy?"

Larcy said calmly, "A personal preference. Good night, Lyn." And went on down the hall to her own room.

What was Lyn doing wandering the upstairs hall? Looking in on David Magnam? What reason did she have?

Moonlight shimmered in through the windows, lay in a bright silver pattern across the floor. Larcy undressed, gave a weary sigh, and climbed into bed.

Chapter Nineteen

WEDNESDAY, as if he was reluctant for her to leave, David Magnam was full of commands and dozens of irrelevant tasks for her to do, so that it was nearly noon by the time she was dressed and on her way downstairs.

She frowned, feeling a moment's irritation. She'd been kept so busy jumping here, there, that she had completely forgotten to phone Pete!

She was looking hesitantly at the phone . . . should she phone Pete now? If she wasted too much time she would certainly miss the bus . . .

The door bell pealed, jarring into her thoughts. She looked up quickly. No one came to the house . . . no one who rang the front door bell.

Larcy walked slowly over to the door and stared through the screen. The man was short, too thin, young, with bold dark eyes, dark hair that grazed the collar of the striped jacket he wore, and a mocking, scornful twist to his mouth that filled her with a vague feeling of familiarity, as if she'd seen him sometime . . . some place.

He eyed her boldly, the mesh of the screen door crisscrossing his features so that it was like looking at a Dali painting. "You wouldn't be the Francis doll, would you?" There was a grating, repulsive sound to his voice.

Larcy looked back at him coldly. "Whom do you wish to see?"

"My, my," he said, in evident scorn, "quite the lady, aren't we?" His voice changed, the veiled threat poking out boldly, "The Pierce dame around? She'd better be."

Larcy stared at him, a flush of anger darkening her cheeks. And then Bena's voice sounded just behind her.

"It's all right, Larcy, you go on and enjoy yourself, I'll take care of this." She gave a quick glance at the young man behind the screen, said carefully, "You're early. I understood the . . . employment office wasn't sending anyone out until afternoon."

He looked back at her, his eyes fierce, angry. "Maybe you've forgot," he said, "I'm Joe Oselie."

Bena wet her lips, shot a nervous glance at Larcy. "No," she said, slowly, "I haven't forgotten." She stretched out a hand to touch Larcy's arm. An imploring gesture? Larcy wondered.

"The yard is such a . . . mess," she told Larcy, giving that wry smile again. "Sybil just doesn't have the time and I thought . . ." Her thin, arched brows raised, saying, in effect, that surely Larcy could understand her reluctance to bring up the yard to Sybil . . . She shrugged, "I phoned the employment office and asked them to send someone over."

The young man scowled, "Listen, lady," he said, his voice menacing, "you ain't getting through to me."

Bena said quickly, giving Larcy what managed to be, almost, a push towards the door, "Go along Larcy

195

dear, or you'll miss your bus. I'll show the young man what's to be done, and have a good time, Larcy."

Larcy found herself on the outside of the screen door, brushing against the young man in the purple jacket as she walked past him.

He needed a bath, a shave, a change of clothes. She did not look up or back, but kept on walking, back straight, purse swinging from her left shoulder.

Joe Oselie, whoever he was, had not been sent over from the employment office. He had not come to do the yard work. Bena had thought that up on the spur of the moment. A yard that held no more than a few spears of grass, that was composed of sand and flagstones, needed little done to it.

The sun, high and bright, beat down on her uncovered head as she walked. A shiver of memory hit her. Of course he'd seemed familiar . . . because she had seen him before. Sitting in the Coney Island that day, talking to Bena!

The sun had dampened her hair. She put up a hand that trembled just the slightest, and lifted the bang off her forehead, wiping the dampness away.

The shiver deepened. He'd been quite threatening when he'd asked to see Bena. There had been no doubt in him but that she'd see him.

Bena had been quite upset to see him. Afraid. It had showed in her face, in the nervous movements of her hands.

Hadn't she known he was coming? Or . . . had he come before he'd been supposed to come? Surprised Bena, leaving her unprepared.

Certainty hit Larcy. Of course, of course. He'd

been supposed to come later in the afternoon . . . after Larcy was out of the house. It was why Bena had asked her to take Wednesday off instead of Thursday. Because he had insisted on seeing her.

But then he'd become impatient and had come earlier than Bena had told him to come. And he'd not been prepared to follow along on Bena's ready excuses.

She bit at her under lip, feeling wretched, miserable. Was he the other blackmailer? The one Bena had mentioned in shocked tones, the one Philip Francis had spoken of in admiring tones, as having the brains?

She reached the highway, waited as the yellow bus made its lumbering way to the side of the highway. She'd see Pete, she thought, talk to him, away from her mother, of course.

Pete would know if she was being silly or not. He'd tell her what to do. She felt a moment of comfort as she climbed aboard the bus, settled into a seat next to the window.

And then a frown creased her forehead, brought doubt and uncertainty. Pete had been impatient with her when he'd left. What was it he'd said . . . ? *She's only being polite . . .* as if she, Larcy, was in the wrong.

She tried to shake off the gloom of her mood. The day was bright and clear, she watched the lake as the bus lumbered its way along the road. It was a morning for sailboats and fishing boats, for swimmers and skiers.

Maybe she and Pete would go to the park and

have a game of tennis. She tried to inject lightness into her thinking. She might even exert herself . . . and surprise him by winning.

She watched a car filled with youths in bathing suits go by in the opposite direction. When she went away . . . and it was not *if* but *when,* she and Pete would have to come to Port Hope for the summer. There simply was not any place like Port Hope in the summer.

A feeling of nostalgia hit her, almost as if she had already gone and the summers and her girlhood were already behind her.

She put up a hand, lifting the bang of hair from off her forehead, letting it drop again.

Her mother was nursing a slight cold. Larcy said, her voice scolding, affectionate, "You've been sitting in front of the fan again, and after I've told and told you . . ."

Her mother sneezed, and Larcy said, automatically, "gesundheit." Her mother blew delicately and moved towards the kitchen, saying over her shoulder that she'd made some fresh cinnamon buns and the coffee should be just about ready.

Larcy got up from the sofa that was slip covered in an early American print and followed her mother into the kitchen saying firmly that they'd have their coffee and buns at the kitchen table.

She got cups and saucers from the cupboard over the sink. "And," she said, "I'll prepare lunch and supper myself and you'll be the one who gets waited on."

Her mother's plump face held a look of horror. "Here I am," she said, in a tone of utter misery, "sick to death with a cold and now I'm being told I have to eat your cooking!"

Larcy grinned. "Your dramatic ability leaves much to be desired," she said cruelly. "It's a good thing father married you, because if you had to make your living being a dramatic actress . . . !" She sighed and rolled her eyes ceilingward.

Her mother sneezed again, said "gesundheit" herself when Larcy didn't say it, sighed and said that she hadn't brought her daughter up to make mockery of her.

Larcy grinned at her and said heartlessly, "you aren't sick to death with a cold, mother darling, and you might as well accept the facts of life, and the facts of life, as of today, are that I'm going to do the cooking and wait on you."

"Oh, my," Mrs. Ryan said, staring down at her coffee which Larcy had poured for her, "the utter mockery of it." And then she lifted her eyes and looked at Larcy, and there was teasing in her gaze.

"It just so happens," she said, smugly triumphant, "that I baked a strawberry pie this morning and have chicken and noodles all ready to be put in the oven and heated."

Larcy grinned, shook her head. "You darling," she said, "if you only knew how I despise my own cooking."

Her mother said, a hint of chiding in her voice, "You'd never take time to let me teach you any more than the elements of cooking."

Larcy buttered a cinnamon bun, said smugly, "It isn't good for people to really enjoy food, because then they get too fat and have all sorts of trouble and . . ."

Her mother watched as she finished her second cinnamon bun. "I've noticed," she said, in a "tongue in cheek" voice, "that you hardly practice what you preach."

Larcy wiped her buttery fingers on a napkin, "does sort of seem that way, doesn't it?" She shot a grin across the table at her mother. "Pete bakes very good bread," she told her. "His mother taught him when he was around nine and he's never forgotten, or so he tells me."

Her eyes searched her mother's face. "I forgot to phone him before I left," she said. "Do you suppose he's at home?"

Her mother shrugged, poured each of them a second cup of coffee. "There's one good way of finding out," she told Larcy. "You can telephone him after you've finished eating."

Larcy was doomed to disappointment because Pete was not at home when she phoned. His mother, sounding very surprised to discover it was Larcy, said, "But you aren't supposed to come home until tomorrow. I'm sure Pete said *Thursday*. He had to take his car to have something done to it, and he said, I heard him tell the garage man that it had to be today because his girl was coming home tomorrow and he . . ."

Larcy cut in gently. "Mrs. Crimmins," she said, "I was supposed to come home tomorrow, but something came up and Mrs. Pierce asked me to take today in-

200

stead." She tried to temper the disappointment in her voice. "Do you think Pete will be back by supper time?"

"I don't know," his mother said, "it does seem to take such an awful long time when he's got someone working on that car of his."

Her voice sounded muffled as if she'd turned away from the phone, then came back strong as she said, "It looks like it's going to cloud up and rain. That could bring him back sooner than expected. I just don't know, Larcy. He did want to have the car fixed and ready. He said he was going to pick you up tomorrow at that place so you wouldn't have to ride the bus in."

She sounded, Larcy thought, almost as if Larcy had let Pete down by coming in a day early. Larcy grimaced, thinking *mothers,* in a mood at once tender and impatient.

"As soon as he comes home," Mrs. Crimmins promised, "I'll have him phone you, Larcy. The very minute."

When Pete was not back by five-thirty, and the clouds his mother had predicted were blanketing the sky, Larcy, heavy hearted and disappointed, decided to leave early.

Her mother, with her eyes on the ugly, threatening skies, and her ears tuned to the radio that intermittently stopped a particular program to issue warnings of violent thunderstorms for the area, offered no objections to Larcy returning early. In fact, she seemed to think it an excellent idea.

201

"I'd never be able to get to sleep," she said, "thinking of you riding that awful bus in a storm."

Larcy cast a doubtful eye at the telephone. There wasn't much hope Pete would be back now before she left. With a sigh, she gathered up her things, combed her hair, applied more lipstick. When she walked out into the kitchen again, her mother informed her blithely that she'd called a taxi.

Larcy stared at her. "It isn't raining yet." She grinned, shook her head. "I didn't know you were such an extravagant woman."

Her mother said complacently, "You're paying for the taxi, you know."

Larcy kissed her. "I want you to go to bed," she told her, "and if your cold gets worse you're to phone me. Promise."

Her mother nodded, and then she cupped Larcy's face in her two hands and said, with a terrible softness, "You're a very good child, Larcy."

Larcy scowled at her. "Now don't you think you can get away with being maudlin just because you've got a bit of a cold." There was a tenderness in her throat.

The bus ride back was bleak and boring, the threat of the storm approaching closer, thunder rumbling across the sky and patches of lightning flashing like firecrackers going off on the Fourth of July.

The rain held off until Larcy reached the back of the house, and then came down in such a violent gush that she was drenched by the time she closed the kitchen door behind her.

Sybil, scouring the sink, turned to say crossly,

202

"You're back. Thought you was to be gone for the day."

Larcy shrugged, said, "I wanted to beat the storm back." She glanced down at her soaked clothing, "I almost managed."

"Larcy!" Bena's voice sounded from the doorway that led into the dining room, "I didn't expect you back so soon."

She sounded upset, Larcy thought. More than upset, frantic. Larcy said, practically apologizing, "It was going to storm, and I knew I'd have to take the bus back . . ."

Bena frowned, "But I thought Pete . . ." she said.

Larcy shook her head. "He wasn't at home. He expected me to come tomorrow."

Bena sighed. "I'm sorry, Larcy." She glanced at Larcy's wet clothing. "You'd better change," she told her, "before you catch yourself a cold."

Larcy shivered. "I'm beginning to think it's a good idea." She hurried out of the room and up the stairs. She couldn't say her return had been an occasion for celebration on either Sybil's or Bena's part.

Since it was still, technically, her afternoon off, she did not put on the stiff nurse's uniform, but slipped into a slim cotton shift and sandals.

She walked into David Magnam's room, saying cheerfully, "Aren't you going to ask me why I came back early? Everyone else has."

He didn't answer her, merely stared up at her out of vague, empty eyes, his breathing sounding heavy and labored, as if it took all of his strength to draw each struggling breath.

Frowning, Larcy touched the tips of her fingers to

the pulse in the thin, flabby wrist and found it rapid and uneven. His condition, although milder, seemed to be a repetition of Tuesday night when Dr. Ule had had to be called.

Still frowning, Larcy went out of the room and downstairs. She could not help but wonder why Bena had not mentioned her father's condition.

Bena was in the dining room gazing out at the rain swept patio. She turned slowly when Larcy said her name. She shook her head at Larcy's look.

"You're worried over father," she said. "I should have mentioned it to you, Larcy, but then you were so wet and cold and bedraggled." She shook her head again, said gently, "I've already talked to Dr. Ule, Larcy. He said there was nothing to do except to give him some of those nitroglycerine tablets and keep him quiet."

Larcy frowned, and then relaxed. The doctor had seen the way he was on Tuesday, and if he wasn't alarmed by this attack . . . Still she frowned. "Did Mr. Magnam do anything unusual this afternoon? Anything . . . active?"

Did Bena look alarmed? Upset? Larcy dismissed the notion. Bena shook her head, looking, sounding, quite calm. "Larcy," she said, with utmost gentleness, "you know father doesn't leave his bed."

Larcy's mouth shook and a stab of fear went through her. She thought of David Magnam as he'd been that afternoon she'd stood watching him from the doorway. The way he'd handled those scissors of his, as if they were a weapon, a knife, drawing his arm back, stabbing, stabbing . . .

She shivered and Bena said, contritely, "Dear Larcy, you've gotten a chill. Go into the kitchen and get warm. Sybil usually has the oven on. Tell her I sent you in there . . ." she gave Larcy a gentle push, "go now."

She came to the kitchen door to say, "Oh, Larcy, if I know you," a gentle laugh, "you're already worrying about father's morphine injection . . ." her smoky eyes searched Larcy's face. "I remembered to ask Dr. Ule about that, and he said you were to go ahead with his medicine as always."

She smiled at Larcy, turned around and disappeared. Sybil slammed the coffee pot down on the burner. "Coffee still left," she said, ungraciously, "maybe a cup'll warm you up."

"Thank you," Larcy said. Why would Dr. Ule say she was to go ahead with the morphine injection, when Tuesday he had said that if she'd given it to him, the condition his heart was in, she . . . could have killed him?

She poured herself coffee when it was hot, sat down at the kitchen table, staring at the wall behind the sink as she drank it. If David Magnam's heart was not slowed down by eight-thirty, she'd phone Dr. Ule herself.

Her hand shook against the handle of the coffee cup as she lifted it to her lips. Was it that she . . . didn't trust Bena?

She was spared making the call, however, because

205

David Magnam seemed to pull out of it by eight o'clock. He glared up at her, weakly but defiantly. "Why are you staring at me like that?"

She shook her head, "I wasn't staring at you."

He frowned, said, "where's that white thing you're supposed to wear? If I'm paying for a nurse. . . ."

Larcy said gently, "I'm still off duty, Mr. Magnam, until nine o'clock."

He continued to glare at her, but did not pursue the subject.

By ten-thirty the storm seemed to have abated, but there was a dark waiting about it, as if it was holding itself in abeyance to strike later on.

Larcy stood at the window. She'd begun to feel drowsy. She turned towards the bed, stifling a yawn, and there came through the stormy darkness, a muffled, far away throb. It was distant, faint, but steady, like a pulse beat.

A boat, Larcy thought, unbelievingly. She turned to look once again, out of the window at the stormy blackness of the lake.

Something moved out there on the lake, faint lights only barely piercing the blackness.

She was puzzled, worried. Why would anyone take a boat out on a storm-threatened lake?

A pleasure ride? Fishing? Such a thought, she knew, was utterly absurd. The only reason anyone would venture out on the lake on a night like this . . . was necessity.

Necessity for moving something . . . someone . . . while the lake was still shrouded in darkness.

Fear pressed icy fingers against her spine. The

chill was very real now. Her thoughts, unbidden, unwanted, went to the dark, untidy young man who had stood at the screen door staring in with bold, mocking, fierce eyes.

Bena had tried to keep Philip Francis from coming to the house, but he had come. And now he was dead. She'd wanted to keep Joe Oselie from coming to the house. But he'd come, unwanted, upsetting Bena, forcing her into lies, subterfuge. And was he . . . now dead?

A shiver shook Larcy, so violent that her whole body trembled. If only she could have talked to Pete.

Chapter Twenty

BY MORNING all traces of the storm had disappeared, except for debris blown up on shore by the wildness of the waves and wind.

Larcy stared out her bedroom window and saw, almost with shock, that the small motor boat was back in its place, tied securely to its launching post.

A frown wrinkled her forehead. Could she have been mistaken? Hadn't it been a boat she'd seen, heard, out there on the lake, after all?

The frown disappeared, and grimness tightened her lips. It had been a boat. She was not mistaken.

She turned slowly from the window, smoothed her soft hair under the stiff nurse's cap, and walked down the sunlit hall to her patient's room.

He was awake, staring up at her as she came around in front of his bed. There was fierceness in his gaze, behind the pain, fierceness and something else . . . something undefinable.

" 'Bout time you got here," he told her. "I've been lying awake here, waiting."

Larcy said calmly, "If you wanted me, Mr. Magnam, you had only to ring."

"And you'd come running. I'll bet you would." And then, as if his bad temper had spent itself, he said weakly, "My arm hurts. It always hurts . . . that damn fool doctor." His eyes narrowed on Larcy's face. He said, "There's other doctors, Ule's a quack, why does Bena hold on to him? Because he goes along with what she's got in mind?"

Larcy protested quietly, "Mr. Magnam, Dr. Ule is a very fine doctor." A small surge of doubt hit her. She said carefully, "Mrs. Pierce phoned him yesterday when your . . . heart began acting up again and he . . ."

David Magnam was regarding her with scornful mockery. "If she told you that," he said, "she lied. The phone was out all yesterday afternoon. She didn't phone nobody."

Larcy turned away to get the wash basin and towels. "I must have misunderstood," she said. "I expect what Mrs. Pierce actually told me, was that she'd tried to get the doctor."

"You didn't misunderstand nothing," he told her coldly. "Bena told you what she wanted you told." He slapped viciously at the wash cloth. "That damn thing's cold!"

Larcy warmed the cloth in the water. She stared down at the rug, not really seeing it. Had Bena Pierce really expected that she'd have given David Magnam the morphine if his heart had been in the same condition it was when she'd come home?

She frowned, shook her head, wrung out the cloth. David Magnam said furiously, "What are you staring at?"

She looked at him, puzzled. "Staring at?" She shook her head again. "I wasn't staring at anything." When he went to push the wash cloth away, she said firmly, "It isn't cold, Mr. Magnum, that's only your imagination."

209

When she went down to fix his breakfast tray, the downstairs was empty, soundless. But when she brought the tray back again, after he'd finished eating, Sybil was in the kitchen and Bena, fully dressed, was sitting at the dining room table, gazing listlessly out of the window.

She turned to smile at Larcy. "Storm's gone," she said. "How is father?"

"As usual," Larcy said. She looked away from Bena, appeared completely engrossed in the tray she carried. "Has the phone been fixed yet, Mrs. Pierce?"

Bena sighed, said wryly, "Oh, dear Larcy, you know about the phone." She sighed heavily. "I should have told you the truth, but you do worry so, and . . ." she shrugged, spreading her hands in a conciliatory gesture, "there was nothing to do." The smoky eyes searched Larcy's now upturned face. She said gently, "I knew that you wouldn't give father the morphine, no matter what I told you. You'd phone Dr. Ule first." She sighed again. "I saw no point in worrying you and so I . . . concocted a lie." She frowned. "Was it such a dreadful thing? Weren't you . . . comforted by it? Was father hurt?"

Larcy could only stare at her. It was such a childish line of reasoning. Coldness pushed its way into her heart. Bena Pierce was not a childish woman.

She said carefully, "Mrs. Pierce, what if I had gone ahead and given Mr. Magnum the injection with his heart still in that condition?"

Bena said, soft, smiling, "But Larcy, I knew you wouldn't."

210

Larcy said desperately, "But what if I had?"

Bena said quietly, "Why then, Larcy dear, I'd have had to tell you, wouldn't I?" She looked around when Lyn, barefooted, her light hair tangled around her face, stomped in from the hall.

There were smudges under her eyes, Larcy noticed, and her young face looked dragged down, as if she had slept little or not at all.

She grabbed the coffee pot before Sybil, coming in with it from the kitchen, could set it down on the table, and poured herself a cup.

She drank it standing up, without sugar or cream.

Bena said, shaking her head at Lyn, "A girl your age should be drinking milk, not black coffee."

Lyn flung a scowl at her. She said fiercely, "I'm not *a girl my age*, I'm me!" She sighed, turned her fierce gaze on Larcy. "Storm keep you awake, too?"

Larcy shook her head. "No," she said. "I'm pretty used to storms."

Lyn lifted her coffee cup to her lips, and over the rim, her brown eyes searched Larcy's face. She said, "Did you think you heard a boat out on the lake last night, Larcy?"

Larcy forced her eyes to look steadily into Lyn's. She said slowly, shaking her head. "A boat? If anyone was caught out on the lake last night in that storm . . ." She gave a very real shudder.

Bena said, "Anyone out in a boat would have pulled into shore long before night came." Her smoky eyes glanced across the table at Lyn, and she said, "You should have combed your hair before coming to the table."

211

Lyn said crossly, "Stop treating me as if I were a child!"

Bena said gently, "How else can I treat you, when you act childishly?" She poured herself a cup of coffee, arched her brows at Larcy. "Coffee?"

Larcy nodded, and carried the tray on into the kitchen. Sybil had fixed a plate of scrambled eggs. Larcy said, "I can take it in for you, if you want."

Sybil handed her the plate. There was a dark stain on the back of her right hand, starting just above her thumb and extending about an inch beyond her wrist bone.

Grease stain? Larcy wondered. From a boat's engine? Her hands trembled as she carried the eggs in to the table, sat down, took a swallow of the coffee Bena had poured for her, almost scalding her throat.

Bena shot her a bright glance which held a spark of fire. "Oh, dear," she said, "you are troubled, aren't you?" She shook her head. "You aren't thinking about what Lyn said, are you? Worrying that someone was trapped out there on the lake last night?"

Larcy shook her head, let her eyes meet Bena's searching gaze. "That would be silly worrying," she said. "For one thing, I don't know anyone was trapped out there. I didn't hear anything except thunder, wind, the waves." She took another swallow of coffee, a smaller one, this time. "Besides, if there had been someone caught out there in the storm, what good would my worrying over it now, do?"

She stared down at her coffee cup . . . Why had she thought it was grease from a boat's engine?

Couldn't it have been grease from the kitchen drain? That was always getting clogged.

Bena switched her gaze to look out the window that faced the patio. "It's a good thing," she said, "that I sent that young man home yesterday. If I'd let him clean the yard, it would have needed cleaning again after the storm."

She turned her gaze on Larcy again. "You are troubled," she said gently. "Is it . . . your boy friend?" Her smile was soft, warm. "It isn't prying, Larcy, dear," she said, "I'm really interested."

Larcy decided there was nothing to do except to play along with Bena. There was a growing knot of fear tightening in her stomach.

"Pete?" she said. "No . . . not really. It's just . . . well, I left my mother coming down with a cold, and Pete was out of town, and the storm and then Mr. Magnam having that upset . . ."

Bena chided gently, "Larcy . . . Larcy . . . You're much too young to let things . . . upset you." She put up a hand, smoothing the silver wing that frosted her dark hair near the tips of her ears. "As a nurse," she said, "you have to learn to . . . accept things. Isn't that true?"

Larcy shrugged, finished her coffee. "Technically," she said. "But even though I'm a nurse, Mrs. Pierce, I'm still a . . . human being."

Bena frowned, said warmly, "Of course you are, dear. Of course." The frown deepened. "I wonder if I should phone the employment agency, have them send over that young man or . . . someone. It isn't only the yard, Sybil says she needs the windows done."

Her eyes lit on Larcy's face. She said, "Johnson's coming home in August." There was a young freshness about her eyes, her mouth. "For good," she said.

Lyn, her back to them, made a scornful sound low in her throat, then said, without turning around, "For heaven's sake, Bena, do you have to sound as if you were still on your honeymoon?"

Her bare feet sounded against the boards of the hall, against the uncarpeted stairs as she raced up the stairs.

Bena stared after her for a moment, and then sighed. She said, "I don't know how . . . Johnson will take Lyn's moods." She sighed again. "He's a man of moods, himself."

She pushed aside her coffee cup and got slowly to her feet.

Larcy watched her move out into the patio, sit down at the redwood table and stare up at the wealth of scrub pine that wound twisted and gnarled up the small hill.

Had there been fright as well as anxiety in Bena's eyes? Larcy sighed, took some of the scrambled eggs that had grown cold, and ate them without any real appetite.

Chapter Twenty-One

THE DAY, bright and cheerful, found no answering cheer or brightness in Larcy. There was a kind of waiting anxiety in her, an ominous certainty of dread and danger lurking in the walls of the house, trailing along the woodwork, closing doors that should have remained opened.

She looked dazedly at Sybil when the maid passed her on the stairs, carrying a scrub pail filled with soapy water.

She said, in answer to Larcy's unasked question, "He spilled something on the rug, and she said I was to scrub it out."

"Oh?" Larcy said, for want of anything else to say. She continued up the stairs and along the hall to David Magnam's room. Sybil had left the door almost closed.

Larcy sighed and pushed it inwards with the heel of one hand, and then stooped down, frowning, as she caught the sparkle of something caught between the edge of the door and the frame.

She dug it out with a fingernail and saw that it was a button, large, flat, a shiny bronze, definitely a man's kind of button.

That was absolutely idiotic, she knew. There was no man living in this house, except for David Magnam and his clothing was limited to pajamas.

And besides, David Magnam would not be outside,

prowling the halls, losing a button. He was a sick, dying, old man who could not leave his bed except with help.

She dropped the button into one of the pockets in her uniform. Sheer terror kept her slender body rigid, tight, so that her movements became automatic.

Who did the button belong to? Philip Francis? Lyn said he'd been upstairs, been in David Magnam's room, talked to him.

Had he been wearing a jacket or suit when he'd been found? She closed her eyes trying to concentrate, to bring up the newspaper accounts, remember what had been said, recall the picture of the body curled up there in the rowboat.

She shuddered and opened her eyes quickly. He hadn't been wearing a jacket . . . Her lips tightened, drew inwards. How could she be so certain? He could have been wearing a jacket and the button could have been loose . . . a man like that would never think to sew on a loose button, and it could have pulled off and dropped onto the floor, and Sybil's vacuuming could have shoved it up against the door.

But then, if he hadn't been wearing a jacket, where would the button have come from? Dr. Ule's suit coat? She shook her head. A man of the doctor's professional standing would not go around wearing a suit coat with a loose button.

Fear moved in little swirls around her. And anyway, the doctor would not be wearing a suit coat or jacket with buttons like the one she'd found, big, flamboyant, oversized buttons.

The kind of buttons that would suit a certain dark,

untidy young man she'd seen peering through the screen on Wednesday?

She tried to jerk herself back to a semblance of sanity as she went on inside the room to face her patient.

It wasn't until she brought up his lunch that she saw the spot near the bed. A dark spot, still wet around the edges, a spot that had not come clean when Sybil had scrubbed it.

She became aware of David Magnam's fixed stare on her bent head.

He said, "What are you staring at on the floor? What's down there?"

She shook her head. "I was thinking that I must have spilled some water out of the basin this morning when I washed you."

He said impatiently, "Damn fool woman had to bring a scrub pail up here, put water all over the rug, because I spilled a bit of glue."

"Oh?" Larcy said, as she'd said to Sybil, because it was all she could think of to say. And then she said carefully, "It will dry, it won't take long." As if she thought he was worrying about the rug being wet.

And she knew that it wasn't worrying him at all. She knew this as she knew that whatever had spilled onto the rug had not been glue.

The glue he used came in a plastic tube, it came out a drop at a time . . . when the tube was squeezed. There was no way that it could have spilled onto the rug.

Her hands were trembling as she took the tray back to the kitchen when he was finished. And what,

217

she asked herself carefully, did she think had caused the stain on the rug which Sybil had not been able to wipe out?

Did she think it was a blood stain? Whose blood? The dishes rattled on the tray as her hands shook. Bright sunlight from the hall window warmed her back as she started down the stairs.

Had somebody been killed in David Magnam's room? Killed and his body dragged, stomach down, through the door and out into the hall? Leaving the stain on the bedroom rug and the button lodged up against the door framing, as silent evidence?

And who did she think had been killed? The young man in the purple striped jacket, with the untidy hair and the bold hating eyes, who had made himself dangerous to Bena?

Philip Francis had made himself dangerous to Bena. And Philip was dead. But the police knew who his murderer was . . . No, no, no. She shook her head violently, as if arguing with herself, the newscast had not said that. It had hinted only that the police had a clue. And it did not even need to mean that. It could have meant no more than that the police were still working on finding the murderer.

The tray felt icy cold against her stiff fingers. The murderer could be here . . . in this very house. Now.

She carried the tray into the kitchen, emptied it, washed out the dishes David Magnam had used.

The kitchen was bright, empty. She could see Sybil out on the patio. The ugly stench of burning garbage stung her nostrils.

Sybil, as if aware of being watched, turned to look toward the house. Larcy walked out of the kitchen, through the long, narrow hall and out the front door, down the three steps and stood on the low rise of sand staring out across the lake, down at the beach.

Sybil burned garbage quite often. Why did the fact that she was burning it this morning worry her? Because she had expected the stench of burning cloth?

She shivered in the warm morning breeze and hugged her arms around her chest as if she was cold. There had been no smell of burning cloth, only the ugly, acrid stench of old garbage.

She drew an unsteady breath and one hand reached into the pocket that held the button, and her fingers closed around it.

If she thought something like . . . murder . . . a violent shiver shook her . . . then her duty, her safety, was to go to the police with her suspicions.

She thought of Lieutenant Bricker, of his cold, shrewd eyes searching her face, of the disbelief in his voice as he'd talked about the *walk* she'd taken alone, at nearly midnight, along the beach.

Might he not believe she was holding something back? Knowing more than she was willing to tell? She bit at her dry underlip.

You were supposed to have something concrete when you went to the police, weren't you? Oh, she didn't know. She didn't know. Confusion shook her, and her fingers closed tighter around the hardness of the button in her pocket. It was something concrete, was it not?

But was it? It could have been dropped days,

weeks ago, and the vacuum had steadily pushed it along the floor of the hall, pressing it closer and closer against the woodwork until finally it had become lodged there at the door.

It could belong to anyone. A vandal who had sought refuge or mischief in the house early in the spring before Bena and her father had come.

An old jacket of Johnson Pierce's Bena had discarded. Was it inconceivable that a man like Johnson, a gambler, a wild, reckless man as both Sybil and Bena had said of him, wouldn't have a jacket with such buttons as the one she had found?

She walked slowly down the rise until her feet hit the sand of the beach. She walked over to the water's edge, leaning down to dip her hand in the water, withdrawing it with a shudder.

She stood for a moment watching the concentration of gulls on the pile of rocks out in the lake. And then slowly, almost as if she was being compelled, she turned to face in the direction of Simms Island.

A wealth of marsh land, uninhabited, unwanted, even by picnickers. She ran her tongue over her dry, trembling lips. The boat she'd heard, seen, the night of the storm. Had its destination been Simms Island?

A fit place to unload an unwanted body? It wouldn't wash up on shore someplace to be identified. It could lay there weeks, months, perhaps even years, before it was discovered. And by that time, it might be almost impossible for anyone to recognize the . . . victim. Especially if all identifying marks had been . . . removed.

She didn't know Lyn had come up behind her until

the girl's young voice said brittlely, "thinking of swimming out to the island, Larcy?"

Larcy, shaking her head, turned around to face Lyn. "Not much," she said. She even managed a light laugh. She let a frown pinch her brows together. "It's queer, isn't it," she said, "that with everybody wanting their own island, nobody wants Simms Island." She shook her head again. "It could be that nobody actually knows about it. I've lived near here for all of my life, and I never even knew it had a name."

Lyn said, shrugging, "Somebody will buy it one day. It could even be Johnson. He likes to take something and make nothing out of it."

Larcy was about to correct her, tell her she'd said it wrong . . . that the way it really was . . . take nothing and make something out of it . . . but then she thought that perhaps Lyn hadn't said it wrong, that she'd said it exactly the way she'd meant it.

Lyn moved on down the beach. Larcy watched her for a moment, she stooped down, lifted some sand in one hand and let it sift through her fingers.

Lyn was sitting on a stone staring out across the lake, when Larcy turned around and walked back to the house.

It was in the afternoon that she knew she was going to phone Pete, and she also knew that she could no longer stay in the house, be responsible for David Magnam's safety.

She hadn't changed from her uniform. She walked slowly scanning the beach for a sight of Pete. He'd sounded impatient with her over the telephone when

221

she'd told him to leave his car at the public beach parking lot and walk down.

She was miserable, unhappy, frightened. What if Pete didn't believe her? What if he thought she was only . . . making everything up?

Still he'd told her, hadn't he, that whenever she was ready to talk about what was bothering her, he'd be ready to listen. But . . . that was before he'd seen Bena Pierce, talked to her.

She drew a quivering breath. Seeing Pete swinging along the edge of the water, head held high, arms hanging loosely, she hurried to meet him.

Pete frowned just the slightest. He said, shaking his head, "Your uniform makes you look different," he said, "calm, efficient . . . not my girl."

Larcy said, and her lips quivered, "I am your girl, Pete."

"Oh?" he said. His eyes were neither gay nor brash nor teasing on her face. He reached down and took one of her hands, his fingers closing warm and secure around hers.

"Tell me about it," he said softly.

"Oh, Pete," she said, "Oh, Pete . . . I'm . . . scared." A shiver shook her, even to the hand that was held so tightly, so warmly, in Pete's grasp.

"Scared of what?" Pete asked her.

Larcy wet her dry lips, she stared down at the sand, scuffling her shoes along in it as she walked. "I don't know," she said, "I don't have any proof, except this," she held out the button to him, "but I think . . . I'm afraid . . . someone was . . . was murdered in my patient's bedroom the . . . the night of the storm."

222

Her eyes turned to look out across the lake, to where Simms Island was a greenish brown blur. "And . . . and the body taken over to Simms Island."

She saw that Pete was staring down at her unbelievingly, as if he thought she'd concocted the story for his benefit.

She said desperately, "Pete, I heard a boat leave shore that night. I saw the lights. And Bena wanted me out of the house on Wednesday which was why she had me take that day off instead of Thursday, and the man came too early so that I saw him, and Bena lied about the reason he'd come and . . . and there's a spot on Mr. Magnam's rug that could very well be . . . blood."

"Whoa," Pete said. "Whoa. You've left me far behind. Let's start at the beginning and take it more slowly."

Larcy shook her head, turning to look towards the house. "There isn't time," she said. "Bena said I could take the boat out any time I wanted to . . . Pete, I want to go to Simms Island. I can tell you about it on the way."

Pete frowned, began slowly shaking his head. "Larcy," he said, "if you think you have anything, then the thing to do is to go to the police with it. I'll go with you."

She shook her head violently. "And have me be wrong about it? And have them laugh at me?" She turned slowly to face him. "Pete," she said, "please humor me in this. If there's nothing on the island then I'll be able to think maybe I've been wrong."

Pete's frown remained. He said, "It could be a dangerous thing, Larcy, if these people really have something to hide." His face darkened. He said, "That man who was murdered, wasn't he found only a short ways from here?"

Larcy said slowly, "He was Mrs. Pierce's brother-in-law. He'd been to see her only the day before."

Pete said firmly, "That settles it. We're not going to that island. We're going to the police. And you're going to get out of that house, and don't tell me about your duty to your patient." His eyes glared on her face. "I don't happen to want you killed."

"Please, Pete," Larcy said. "This is something I have to do. If you won't go with me, I'll go myself."

"All right," he said, slowly, "all right, but I think you're wrong."

Larcy wondered, as she and Pete pushed the boat out into the water, started the motor, if Bena or Lyn or Sybil was watching from one of the windows in the house. Watching and . . . knowing what was in her mind.

She shivered and brushed a hand across her face. Pete glanced up at her, but said nothing. He neither laughed nor smiled, but stared straight ahead, a worried, anxious air about him.

Larcy touched his shoulder and said, in a low, tight voice, "Pete, I shouldn't have gotten you into this."

He said carefully, "But I am in, Larcy, and so are you." He sighed, stared out across the lake. "I only hope it's a wild goose chase."

224

Larcy thought, "So do I." But there was this feeling in her, like a certainty, a dread, that they were going to find a body on the island. Coldness sliced through her. She wanted to reach out and hold onto Pete, but he seemed strangely aloof.

She sat huddled in the prow of the boat, listening to the chug of the motor. She'd promised to tell Pete all of it, from the beginning, but he seemed not to want to talk, and it was a silent, anxious trip across to the island.

Pete did say once, without even looking at her, "The police are pretty thorough, Larcy. Sometimes they work slowly and it seems as if they aren't doing anything, but they're doing something."

Larcy stared at his back. She said, "What are you telling me? That I shouldn't have tried this on my own?"

Pete nodded. He said, "That's what I'm telling you."

He pulled the boat up on the sand, threw out the anchor, stood for a moment staring around. Larcy, at his side, stared, too. She said slowly, "Lyn wasn't telling any lie. It is a pretty grim looking place."

Pete said, "It's not exactly the spot I'd pick for my vacation." He looked at the waving marsh grass not too far inland from the tiny beach. "Duck hunters probably like it," he said.

There was sand under their feet, and then the wetness of the marsh. It seemed to Larcy that fog came up from under the waving grass and hung like an impenetrable curtain. But there was no fog, and the sky above the island was blue and bright.

225

She shivered and dug her hand tighter into Pete's as they walked. She wished now she had not persuaded Pete to bring her here.

There was a curiously pregnant silence, a watching kind of waiting. Larcy moved her hand in Pete's. She said, "I'm sorry we came. Let's go back. I was wrong to think we should come here."

She was aware suddenly that Pete had stopped walking, that he'd pulled her back, so that she was standing, not beside him, but a short ways behind him.

He said, a tight, hard note in his voice, "You came looking for a body, Larcy. And . . . there it is."

Larcy opened her eyes wide, stared blankly at the toe of the exaggeratedly pointed shoe that extended out from a covering of marsh grass and pine branches, twigs, bits of brush, at the hand that trailed limply along the ground that was not sand here, but mud, oozy and wet, slime.

She turned and buried her face in Pete's shoulder. When she would have looked again, he would not allow her. She said, slowly, heavily, "I have to look. I have to see . . . who it is."

He released her and she stepped forward, bent down, lifted aside the grasses, and looked down into the thin, dark, mocking face of Joe Oselie.

Something caught in her throat, she straightened, whirled, to press herself tightly against Pete. She'd known whose body she was looking for. All along she'd known, and yet there was something inexorably frightening in the knowledge that she'd found it.

Chapter Twenty-Two

"IT DOESN'T seem right," Larcy said, "to . . . leave him."

Pete's steps towards the boat were hurried, forceful. He said, "Be reasonable, Larcy, there's nothing we can do for him, nothing anyone can do."

He turned when they reached the boat to glance at her. "Who," he asked quietly, "is . . . was . . . Joe Oselie?"

Larcy shook her head. She said slowly, not looking at him. "I don't really know. Not for sure. I think he was . . . the second blackmailer. I saw him and Mrs. Pierce talking together in Port Hope. She had . . . sent me to do some errands she said were . . . immediate, necessary, had to be done that very morning. Only it wasn't true. That they had to be done, I mean."

She took a steadying breath. "And then he came on Wednesday and she said . . . Mrs. Pierce . . . that he was from the employment office, that she'd asked for someone to be sent over to do the yard. Only the yard didn't need doing, and he was angry and . . . and impatient with her, and he didn't know at all what she was talking about."

When she stopped for breath, Pete said carefully, "How do you know he was blackmailing her? And if he was the second blackmailer, who was the first one?" He drew in his breath, frowned, and said with dread certainty, "That man who was killed at Stalen Pier, Mrs. Pierce's brother-in-law."

"Yes," Larcy said, in a small, tight voice. "I . . . overheard him and Mrs. Pierce talking down on the beach. This Philip Francis said . . . he said that this other man was the . . . the brains of the job, and he wasn't satisfied with . . . with five hundred dollars, he said, he called it 'chicken feed.'"

She climbed into the boat. Pete was having trouble with the motor, but at last he had it going. The sun beat down bright and hot, the smell of the marsh was in her nostrils.

"Pete," she said slowly, "do you think Mrs. Pierce killed them both? She is very much in love with her husband and if Philip Francis and Joe Oselie were blackmailing her because of something her husband had done, and she knew he was in danger why I think . . . I truly do think that she could, would, have killed for him."

Pete shook his head, "I don't know, Larcy," he said. "I'm not a detective. I'm just trying to be a lawyer." He frowned at her.

She stared out at the water. "It's such a puzzling thing," she said, "all of it. Mr. Magnam sometimes . . . thinks Mrs. Pierce hired me to kill him." She shook her head at Pete's glance. "He really does," she said. "And he had that awful spell on Wednesday and Mrs. Pierce told me she'd phoned the doctor and it was all right for me to give him the morphine, but the phone was out of order and she could not phone anyone. And if I'd given him the morphine when his heart was acting up, I could have . . . killed him."

Pete's frown deepened. He said unbelievingly, "And you let this kind of stuff keep happening and did nothing about it?" He shook his head, glared fiercely at her. "I thought you had some sense, Larcy."

She said unhappily, "Pete, she did catch a rat, Sybil did. She wasn't lying about it, and I . . . thought she was . . . I don't know exactly what I thought. But don't you see, if I was wrong about there being a rat, I could have been wrong about the other things too, and I didn't want to involve anyone in something that was no more than my overworked imagination."

Pete said nothing, just kept frowning and staring out across the lake. Larcy said miserably, "I tried to talk to you, Pete, I wanted to tell you, but you were always gone."

Pete said slowly, "I'm not going to make you feel any better by telling you that you did right, because you didn't, Larcy. You acted very childishly and foolishly."

Larcy didn't answer him. She said, thoughtfully, "There's one thing I can't understand at all. This newspaper clipping Mr. Magnam lost. Both Bena and Sybil lied about it. It disappeared and I can't understand . . . if the man *was* Mrs. Pierce's husband . . . and if he had been accused of killing his first wife, then if Mr. Magnam knew about it, why would it be important?"

Pete stared at her. He said, "Don't tell me anything more, Larcy. Keep it to tell the police. The more you say, the madder I become. How could you have placed yourself in such a position and then done nothing about it?"

He shook his head, and looked anxiously down at the motor. "Don't tell me that thing's going to act up."

Larcy asked in a thin, small voice, "Do you think Lieutenant Bricker is going to be very angry with me?"

Pete said, "He's going to be mad as hell. And you'll probably be lucky if he doesn't think up some reason for putting you in jail for a good, long spell."

Before his voice died away, the motor gave a series of grunts, then stopped completely.

Pete bent for a look. When he lifted his head, he looked older, sterner. He said, "I don't know too much about motors, but I'm fairly sure this one was tampered with. It looks to me like a pin's been sheared off." His eyes traced Larcy's face. "You weren't supposed to get back to the mainland." There was a sudden note of authority in his voice that was new to Larcy. "Who," he asked her, "knew you were going to take the boat to the island?"

Larcy stared at him, began shaking her head. "No one," she said. "No one could have known. I . . . ." Something caught in her throat. . . . The sun rolled down, hot and bright, she looked behind her at Simms Island, perhaps a quarter of a mile away, at the shiny gleam of the sandy beach, at the greenish-brown jungle of growth. She wet her dry, parched lips and a shadow of fear stirred in her.

"Lyn," she said, her voice low, tense. "Lyn could have . . . guessed." She thought of the way Lyn had come up behind her, on soft feet so that she hadn't known she was there, until her voice had

230

sounded. Of the way she had said, *Thinking of trying to swim to the island?*

A frown creased her forehead. "It doesn't make sense, Pete." She waved her hand, taking in the expanse of water, the closeness of the shore. "Even if I'd been alone, it wouldn't be a desperate situation. A boat is bound to come along." She shook her head, the frown deepening. "What would anyone have hoped to . . . gain by tampering with the boat? Delay? Delay for what?"

Pete shook his head in answer. "I don't know," he admitted. The muscles of his jaws tightened. "It probably wasn't planned thinking, but the result of desperation." He glanced up at the sky. "It's getting hotter," he said, wiping his forehead. "If that boat you were talking about doesn't come along shortly, we'll have to chance a swim back to the island. At least we could find a spot of shade there."

Larcy gave a shudder. "I don't want to go back there, Pete. I don't want to have to . . . think about . . . what's back there."

Pete didn't offer her too much sympathy. He said, "Just remember, Larcy, you got yourself in this mess. If you'd gone to the police . . ."

Larcy's voice sounded small and shaken. "Please, Pete," she said, not feeling at all calm or efficient, even if she was wearing her nurse's uniform, "don't . . . be cross with me."

Pete looked at her and his face softened. He reached across and touched the tip of her nose, gently, lightly. "All right," he said. "I promise."

231

Time went by, twenty-five minutes, thirty-five minutes, forty. The heat of the sun increased. Larcy and Pete trailed their hands in the cold water, splashed it over their heads, their faces, made cups of their hands and let it run down their parched throats.

Pete said finally, "This is no good, Larcy. We're going to have to swim back to the island. The way it is now, someone looking out from shore and seeing us will figure we only dropped anchor to fish awhile."

Larcy stared bleakly at him. His voice softened. He said, "With the boat empty, it's going to be noticed more readily. We'll find shade on the island, and we'll set up a signal. It's the only way."

He looked away from Larcy, said quietly, "You'll have to take off that uniform you're wearing. You can't possibly swim wearing it."

Larcy looked at him blankly, and then down at herself. He was right, she thought. She'd have to take off the uniform. This was no time to stand on her modesty.

She nodded and began slowly unbuttoning the first button. Her eyes were downcast, not looking at Pete, not looking at anything except the slow, awkward movement of her fingers.

Pete said, "You can stop what you're doing, Larcy. There's a boat coming. A Coast Guard patrol boat."

It took a second for his words to sink in. And then she lifted her head, stared at him, and then at the small launch making its swift way towards them.

She began quickly rebuttoning her uniform. She combed one hand through her hair that hung wet and dripping and limp against her face.

232

Pete was standing up, waving wildly. When the patrol boat came alongside, she suddenly dissolved into tears. It didn't help at all when she saw that one of the figures standing in the prow of the boat was the young detective, Lieutenant Bricker.

He stared at her, his eyes sharp, bright, accusing. He said, "Out on a fishing trip, Miss Ryan?"

Slowly, miserably, Larcy shook her head. She said, "Something . . . something's wrong with the motor. Pete . . . said it looks like someone . . . tampered with it."

His eyebrows raised, but other than that, his thin face didn't change. "And why," he asked, his eyes going to Pete, "would you think that?"

Pete shrugged. "I don't know why I think it," he said, his lips firming, thinning, "except that's the way it looks to me, like someone deliberately fixed that motor."

The detective's gaze swept back to Larcy. He said carefully, "Why do you think someone would want to tamper with the motor, Miss Ryan?"

Larcy said fiercely, "Because they knew there was a body on Simms Island, and they . . . knew I was going there, or at least suspected it, and they didn't want the . . . body to be found by anyone."

Her lips quivered. She said, "You aren't to blame Pete. I . . . I made him come with me. He said I should go to . . . the police, only I wanted to make certain before I did that and . . ."

He sighed and shook his head. "Why do some people always think they can work better than the

233

police?" He frowned at Pete, said, "Why didn't you make her follow through on your suggestion?"

Pete didn't smile. He said, "Nobody makes Larcy do anything. She'd very well have gone herself if I'd refused to go along with her idea."

The detective shrugged, looked crossly at Larcy. He said, carefully, deliberately, "If you'd only waited a little longer, Miss Ryan, we'd have found the body for you."

Larcy wiped a hand childishly across her eyes. She said, "you knew about the body being there?"

He said grimly, "We work slowly, Miss Ryan, and we don't broadcast our findings until we are sure of them. Not even to the newspaper." His eyes bored into hers. He asked, "Do you know whose body it is?"

Larcy said, "A Joe Oselie. At least that's what he called himself to Mrs. Pierce when he came to see her on Wednesday."

Lieutenant Bricker said slowly, "He came to see her? Do you know why he came?"

Larcy said, "Mrs. Pierce said he was from the employment office, that she'd asked them to send someone over to fix up the yard, only it wasn't true . . . I could tell by the way that he acted."

"And just why do you think he came?" the detective asked carefully.

Larcy said, staring down at her hands, twisting and untwisting in her lap, "I think he was . . . blackmailing Mrs. Pierce. That other man who was . . . killed, Philip Francis, he was also . . . blackmailing her."

She unclenched her hands, wiped one of them down

her dripping, heat soaked face. She said, "Could we . . . talk about it someplace else? It's so . . . so hot here."

He nodded, his face grim. "We have to pick up the body," he said. There was sarcasm in his voice, "Thanks to your efforts, Miss Ryan, we know for certain now that there is a body. And then we'll talk. It seems you have a lot to tell me." There was ice in his voice, steel. "This time," he told her, "I want all of it, no holding back. You aren't the police, Miss Ryan, and you had no right trying to act as if you were. It was your job to nurse your patient, not to take on the extra job of acting detective."

Larcy nodded, feeling a sense of relief that now it was taken out of her hands, now there was no question of whether or not she should involve anyone or not involve them.

The transferring of Larcy and Pete to the patrol boat, and the lashing of the motor boat to the Coast Guard boat took only a matter of minutes.

The cabin was relatively cool. Larcy sat on one of the bunks and slowly, carefully, interrupted sometimes by questions fired briskly at her from Lieutenant Bricker, talked on and on, remembering, forgetting, going back and retelling the parts she'd forgotten in the first telling.

Pete sat staring blankly at her, as if he could not believe she had let it all happen.

Larcy wished he wouldn't look at her like that, she wished he'd understand.

When she was finished, the detective shook his

235

head, sighed, said, "Well, Miss Ryan, you've come up with quite a fancy tale. Unbelievable, in fact."

He stared down at his shoes, stretched his legs, seeming cramped by the smallness of the space. His head jerked up and he blazed at her, "Exactly what significance do you think this clipping that disappeared, has to the murder of Philip Francis and Joe Oselie?"

Larcy flushed. He didn't believe her. He was . . . making mockery of her. She said fiercely, "I don't know." She bit hard at her under lip to stop its trembling. She said, anger in her voice, "There was a clipping. It wasn't pasted into Mr. Magnam's scrapbook, it did disappear and both Mrs. Pierce and Sybil, the maid, lied about it. I'm sure of that."

The flush darkened on her face. She said, "You've no right to . . . laugh at me, act as if I've merely made up a story for your . . . attention."

He shook his head, said softly, "Believe me, Miss Ryan, I'm not laughing at you. I'm merely trying to fit the pieces together with what I already know, and make a legitimate case, a perfect jigsaw puzzle, if you please." He leaned closer to Larcy, his brows creased in a frown of concentration.

He said carefully, "If this Ronald J. Pierce is the Johnson Pierce to whom Mrs. Pierce is married, and if her father knew . . . and it seems logical if she's been married to him all of these years, that he would know . . . why would the clipping be important enough to be stolen and destroyed?"

Larcy shook her head. "I don't know. I've thought and thought about it."

He went on smoothly, as if there had been no interruption, "I'm led to believe that Ronald J. Pierce and Johnson Pierce are one and the same, and that it is this knowledge that the blackmailers had and were using."

Larcy said, "But if Mr. Magnam knew, why would anyone want to steal the clipping?"

He shook his head, said quietly, "I'll let Mrs. Pierce give me the answer to that." He looked away from Larcy, and then back at her. "The body will be taken on to Port Hope," he said, "and the morgue. But you and I, Miss Ryan, are going to have a long talk with Mrs. Pierce and with your patient."

Larcy's eyes widened on his face. "With Mr. Magnam?" she said. "But he's ill, I don't think the doctor would want you to . . ." she broke off the sentence, shook her head, frowned. "The blood on the rug," she said. She wet her lips, made a choking sound low in her throat. "If . . . he was killed in that room, then you think he . . . Mr. Magnam would have seen . . . known who had done it." It wasn't a question, but a statement of fact.

Lieutenant Bricker said quietly, "It won't take long to find out if the spot is blood, and if it is . . ."

Larcy stared down at her trembling hands. She broke in with the question, because she could no longer hold it inside of her. She said, "Did Mrs. Pierce . . . murder both of those men?"

Somehow she did not want to believe that Bena Pierce had done . . . murder.

She glanced up to see the detective shaking his head. "She didn't kill Philip Francis," he said, "we

237

know Joe Oselie killed him. Probably because they quarreled over how much blackmail was to be asked for, and how it was to be divided. Joe Oselie has had a police record since he was eleven years old. It wasn't hard to tie him up with this case."

He stretched his legs again. "As for his killing," he said, "if the spot proves to be blood, and the blood happens to match that of Joe Oselie, then it's going to be more or less easily proved that he was killed in that bedroom, quite possibly by some one in the house."

Larcy's stomach knotted, turned over, knotted again. She dug both of her hands deep into her pockets, and her left hand closed over the button she'd picked up off the hall floor earlier. She pulled it out, handed it to the detective, said, "I found this lodged up between the door and the door frame this morning."

He took the button, got to his feet and walked out of the small cabin, stooping as he went under the door. When he returned there was a grim smile on his thin, no longer boyish lips. "The button," he said, "matches the ones on the jacket Joe Oselie is wearing."

Larcy caught her breath sharply. It must be Bena, it had to be Bena. She felt sick, lost. She looked at Pete, said to the detective, but looking at Pete, "Can Pete come with me?"

Pete said, looking at her, but speaking to the detective, "He couldn't stop me."

Chapter Twenty-Three

LYN WAS the first to see them. She stared at Larcy with her limp hair, her burnt, hot face, her bedraggled uniform. The brown eyes went from Larcy to the grim faced detective, to Pete, tired, sunburned, fierce eyed.

She said, "Well, for heaven's sake, if the three of you don't look as if you've been to somebody's funeral and then left to find your own way back."

In spite of her flippant voice, Larcy could swear there was fear wary and hidden behind her eyes.

There was silence, heavy and meaningful as they all stared back at her. And then Lieutenant Bricker said in a low, controlled voice, "Why did you tamper with the boat's engine, Miss Francis? Because you knew Miss Ryan was going to Simms Island and you didn't want her there, because Joe Oselie's body was hidden there? Did you hide it there, Miss Francis? Did you kill him?"

Lyn stared at him blankly, and then screamed at him wildly, "I didn't. I didn't. You can't say I did!" She whirled and ran blindly up the stairs and there was the fierce slamming of her bedroom door, as if she thought by the very violence of the sound she could shut out the words the detective had said to her.

There was movement, sudden, flurried, and then

there was Bena Pierce standing at the head of the stairs, looking unhappy, wary, frantic.

Her voice, unlike her eyes, was calm. She said, lifting her mouth so that her lips twisted in a half smile, "Just what is it Lyn didn't do?"

She came slowly down the stairs, tall, slender, proud, her high heels making little clippity, cloppity sounds.

The three of them watched her descent. Lieutenant Bricker said softly, "She didn't kill Joe Oselie."

Larcy saw the panic, quickly veiled, in Bena's smoky eyes, heard the sharp intake of breath that betrayed her, before she said in a shocked, unbelieving voice, "Why would she say that? Why would you think . . ." she shook her head, her eyes moving back and forth from Larcy's face to Pete's, to the detective's, staying there.

"Who is this person?" she asked him, "This Joe Oselie?"

"He was the man who killed Philip Francis," the detective told her calmly.

Larcy saw Bena stand very still on the last step, saw her eyes widen, the terrible whiteness of her face.

Lieutenant Bricker said, "So you didn't know that? Did you think we thought you had killed him? If we'd thought that, we'd have had you in custody before now." He waved a hand in the direction of the living room. "Suppose we all go in and sit down, Mrs. Pierce. We'll all be more comfortable. I have quite a few questions to ask you."

He looked up the stairs, said quietly, "But first, perhaps you'd better tell Miss Francis to come down."

Bena turned her head, followed his gaze. "She wouldn't listen to me," she said.

The lieutenant lifted his voice so that it was no longer quiet, soft, but loud, carrying, so that it went up the stairs, trembled along the hall. He said, "Very well, if she refuses to come down, the only thing left is for me to issue a warrant for her arrest."

Bena Pierce's eyes were wide and disbelieving on his face. Larcy gasped and stared at him. It was Bena whose voice stumbled out the words, "Arrest for what?"

He said low, his voice, grim, uncompromising, "As an accessory after the fact of murder." His nice blue eyes held ice. "She did see the body being moved, Mrs. Pierce. She did tamper with the boat's engine when she suspected Miss Ryan was going to Simms Island."

Bena said desperately, "That proves nothing. It was a child's thinking." She shook her head. "Larcy isn't champion, but she can swim. It was broad daylight. She wouldn't have drowned. Eventually someone would have spotted her, gone after her."

He said quietly, "We'll get to Miss Francis later on. Right now it's you I want to question. Let's go sit down, please, Mrs. Pierce."

The living room was bright, sunshiny. Heat poured in from the opened windows, a slight breeze with the tang of the lake, a wasp buzzed, caught in the folds of the curtains in the big window that overlooked the lake.

Bena sat down on the tan sofa, crossing her delicate ankles gracefully, folding her hands, carefully

241

focusing her gaze on the detective who sat in an arm chair across from her.

Larcy sat down awkwardly on the far end of the sofa, leaving a large gap between her and Bena. Pete drew up a straight backed chair beside the sofa arm, and sat down. He reached out, and for just a moment Larcy felt the firm, warm, reassuring pressure of his fingers, and then he withdrew his hand and sat quietly, not looking at any of them, staring thoughtfully down at the patterned rug.

The detective concentrated his gaze on the wasp, watching its desperate struggles to free itself of the trap in which it was caught.

The sound of the buzzing changed as the wasp moved out from the curtain, lifted itself against the screen, changed its mind and circled the room near the ceiling.

And then slowly, deliberately, the detective faced Bena Pierce. He asked, "Why were you being blackmailed, Mrs. Pierce? Please don't bother to deny you were being blackmailed. We know that you were." He sighed, put the tips of his two hands together, forming an arch and stared at it. "Why didn't you come to the police, Mrs. Pierce, when your brother-in-law came to you asking for money?" His sigh deepened. "You would have prevented two murders."

Bena stared at him bleakly, and then leaned back against the sofa, as if she'd been caught in a trap as had the wasp, and could not find a way in which to extricate herself.

She sighed, closed her eyes, opened them again. "Yes," she said, "Philip was blackmailing me. As you know, or say you know, I didn't kill him." She stared down at the black stripes in her white dress, smoothed the skirt over her thighs. "I didn't kill Joe Oselie, either, lieutenant."

She turned her head to look at Larcy, turned away again. "He came here on Wednesday, I suppose Larcy has already told you that. He . . . he'd phoned me, threatened to go to . . . certain people, unless I got the money for him." She bit at her under lip, and Larcy saw a tiny spot of blood stain where her white, strong teeth had borne down.

"He wasn't like Philip . . . content with a small amount. I talked him into coming out here that afternoon. I sent Larcy away," she shook her head sadly, "but he wouldn't wait. He had to come early." She smoothed the skirt of her dress again, then pleated it between her fingers. "I told him that a thousand dollars was the best I could do. I finally persuaded him, but I told him he'd have to wait, that I couldn't just go into a bank and have them hand me over the money. I told him it would take a little time to borrow that amount."

She brushed a hand over the smooth sides of her hair. "He didn't want to wait. He said he'd go to my father. I tried to stop him. I told him my father was a very sick man, I told him that even if he wasn't sick, it would do him no good, that father was not the kind of man who would pay out money in order to save anyone . . . excepting himself . . . from hurt."

She stared across the room at the detective, who was quietly watching her. "I couldn't stop him," she said. "He brushed past me and went upstairs."

The room held only the quiet sound of their breathing. The wasp hidden somewhere in the room, was quiet, as if it too, listened. The waves moved only gently against the sandy shore.

Bena Pierce sighed, got to her feet, turned to stare up at the picture of her husband that hung above the mantel. She said, "For a few minutes I just stood, not really believing he'd gone upstairs to father's room. And then I went outside. I tried to think, to plan what I must do." She ran a hand nervously across her trembling lips. "I even had a thought of going up to father, begging him for the money. But then I remembered the way he'd . . . laughed at me when I'd gone to him asking him for that clipping . . ."

She turned her head slowly, to look at Larcy, sighed, said, "I knew he'd use it to hurt Lyn. I don't know how he got it, maybe Philip got it to him." She pleated the skirt of her dress again, stared down at her hands. "I was trying to find it that night you heard my door creak . . ." she looked up at Larcy. "I knew you were . . . suspicious," she sighed again, "I had Sybil set out traps, told you she'd seen a rat in the kitchen." She gave a hollow laugh. "It was . . . funny in a way, because, you see, there really was a rat."

She let go of her skirt, clasped her hands in her lap. "I only wanted to destroy the clipping," she said, looking earnestly at Larcy. "You see, what father would tell Lyn wouldn't be half so effective as what he could . . . show her." She wet her dry lips. "If you read only the headlines, Larcy, then you wouldn't know that a . . . child was mentioned, a . . . lit-

244

tle girl. Lyn would have put the pieces together very easily. She'd have . . . known and been hurt by . . . the knowing. Father would have . . . enjoyed that."

The sudden, almost complete, silence of the room was broken by the racing sound of Lyn's footsteps coming into the room, to brake to a stop in front of Bena, and her voice, loud, ugly, fierce, shouting at Bena, "What would I have known?"

For a moment it looked as if she was going to lean down, shake Bena violently. But then she straightened, and only her flushed face, her glaring eyes showed the wildness of her emotion.

Bena's smoky eyes held the brilliance of unshed tears. Her eyes turned from Lyn's to the picture again above the mantel. Very carefully she turned around, went over and sat down again on the tan sofa.

She looked at the detective, said unhappily, "You'll find it all out, won't you, Lieutenant," and then not waiting for his answer, she sighed, said slowly, sadly, "By wanting to keep it a secret, it has caused two murders. Perhaps it's best that it . . . be told."

Lyn whirled around, went over and stood in front of Bena. She said fiercely, "It's me, isn't it? It wasn't Johnson who was being blackmailed, it was you. Because I'm . . . illegitimate and you didn't want Johnson to find out." Her eyes glared fiercely into Bena's. "Marian knew, didn't she? Only Marian wasn't the kind who would tell, even if it would help her. Even if she . . . wanted Johnson for herself."

Bena looked sad, the tears came and held in her smoky eyes. She said slowly, "Marian never wanted

Johnson, Lyn. Only you. She . . . my poor sister . . . she really loved Philip. Always. Forever." She sighed, looked away from Lyn and then back again.

The wasp had begun buzzing again, circling around and around, searching for a way out, an escape. "It wasn't you," she said. "You aren't . . . my daughter, Lyn. You're . . . Johnson's."

Lyn gasped, stared speechless down at Bena. Finally she found her voice, said fiercely, "it's not true. You're lying."

Bena said slowly, heavily, as if the telling hurt her. "Johnson has always liked to gamble. It's like a . . . kind of disease with him. He was always in debt. It was one of the . . . many things that broke up him and his wife." She looked up at Lyn. "It was during one of the many breaks between them that . . . your mother . . . Johnson's wife . . . was found . . . dead. You, Lyn, were three years old at the time. Johnson was . . . embarrassingly in debt. Your mother's death was . . . under suspicious circumstances. Johnson was arrested, held for trial. The biggest motive against him was that he needed money. When it was discovered that his wife's insurance would barely cover her funeral expenses, he was tried and . . . acquitted.

"But the case had made headlines. There were . . . there always are . . . people who form their own opinions, and Johnson saw what that kind of publicity . . . could do to his daughter." She brushed a hand vaguely across the side of her face. "He'd known my sister for a long time. Marian loved children. She'd always wanted children of her own. He

246

turned Lyn's" (she was looking now at the detective) "care over to my sister. He'd always intended making a home for Lyn when he got settled in some other city. But he found it wasn't easy to get a job, the kind of job, at least, that would pay enough to take care of Lyn properly.

"About a year after his wife's death, he joined the navy, liked it, decided to make it his career. He called himself Johnson Pierce, rather than Ronald Pierce. No one connected him with that other Pierce, and in a year most people had completely forgotten all about it.

"Marian and he . . . talked it over together and decided that for Lyn's sake, it would be best if he let well enough alone, that if he was to suddenly appear on the scene as Lyn's father it might only . . . confuse and . . . upset her."

Lyn said wildly, "Of all the crazy, impossible, awful things to do!" Her lips trembled. "All these years when I've thought I was alone, that nobody really cared." Her mouth worked convulsively. "And then when you first came I used to tell myself you were my mother. I . . . wanted to believe that. But when you never would . . . acknowledge me, I told myself I . . . hated you." The tears ran down her cheeks. "But I never could hate you . . ." She drew in her breath, said fiercely, "I'll never forgive him. Never. Never. Never!"

Bena said unhappily, "It was a mistake. A dreadful mistake. I should have seen it."

Lieutenant Bricker said softly, looking at Lyn's back, causing her to have to turn and look at him,

247

"You thought Bena had killed Joe Oselie, didn't you? That's why you wanted to try and keep Miss Ryan from going to the island. You'd seen her move the body, hadn't you?" His voice softened, "Did you help her carry it down the steps, load it into the boat?"

Lyn stared blankly at him, wet her lips, turned to stare at Bena. "I . . . I . . ." she said.

Bena said softly, "No, Lyn didn't help me . . . No one did. I . . . did it alone."

The detective shook his head. "No," he said, "You couldn't have done it alone. You had to have help."

Sybil suddenly was there in the doorway. She said, her eyes flat and still on Bena's face. "I helped her move it. Somebody had to help her. And I knew she hadn't killed him."

"How did you know that?" the detective flung at her.

Sybil shook her head. "I knew it," she said, "because she couldn't kill anybody. And if she was to kill anybody it would be that one upstairs, throwing things up to her, mocking her, walking over her. If she'd have killed him, she'd have had money enough to pay off a dozen blackmailers."

The detective switched his gaze to Lyn, his eyes sweeping her face, his voice soft, even. He said, "You thought Mrs. Pierce had killed him. Why, Miss Francis? Because you . . . saw it?"

Lyn shook her head frantically. "No," she said, "no." And then in a small, unhappy voice. "Who else was there? I hadn't done it. Sybil hadn't. Larcy

248

was away. There was no one else in the house to do it."

Something pushed against Larcy. A pounding, nagging something. It wasn't true. There was someone else in the house. *David Magnam!*

But even as she had the thought, her mind sought to dismiss it. He was helpless. Bedridden. How could a man like that commit . . . murder? But he was suspicious, bitter, hating. If prodded into a wild fury, could he not have had the strength to lunge from his bed, stab Joe Oselie to death?

She frowned. Hadn't she seen him practicing with the scissors, using them as a weapon? Hadn't seen him on two occasions when he'd used his heart more than he should have? Once when he'd nearly died? And . . . hadn't the last time been on the day Joe Oselie had been . . . murdered?

She turned suddenly and looked at the detective. She said, slowly, almost reluctantly, "There was . . . Mr. Magnam." She looked unhappily into the detective's doubting face, told him about the afternoon she'd walked into his room, seen him using the scissors as a knife, stabbing, stabbing, at an unseen foe.

"Exertion," she said, "could have caused his heart to pound."

"Exertion caused by . . . stabbing a man?" The detective continued to look doubtful.

Bena said slowly. "My father is a . . . very sick man. Not only physically. He has always feared that . . . one of us . . . wanted his death." She shook her head. "I found Joe Oselie's body in . . . father's

249

room. On his back. He was dead. Father was . . . asleep, pretending to be asleep."

The detective asked carefully, "And you, Mrs. Pierce, are saying that you think your father, a dying, helpless old man, killed him?"

Bena spread her hands. "I'm saying . . . nothing," she said, "except . . . I didn't kill him." She looked hopelessly at him. "But what jury would believe me?" she asked him.

Larcy didn't look at Pete. She stood up suddenly, "Please," she said, "let me . . . try to get him to admit to it?" She shook her head helplessly, "It's the . . . only way, lieutenant." Fiercely, "You don't want someone to be . . . punished for a crime they . . . didn't do, do you?"

Pete said, "You're not going to do it. I won't let you!"

Larcy said, as she'd said to him other times, "I have to, Pete. I have to."

Chapter Twenty-Four

DAVID MAGNAM was lying quietly in bed, but his eyes were wary. "Who's down there?" he asked Larcy.

"A detective," she told him. "They found the body of that man who was here yesterday. He . . . thinks Mrs. Pierce killed him, because he was blackmailing her."

Larcy saw the smug look that touched David Magnam's lips. She said softly, "but Mrs. Pierce didn't kill him, did she, Mr. Magnam? It was you, wasn't it? You stabbed him with the scissors. You thought he had come to . . . kill you. You were afraid, weren't you? And when he . . . turned his back, you caught up the scissors you keep under your pillow and you . . . lunged at him, killed him. And then you pretended to be asleep when Mrs. Pierce came up and saw the . . . body."

She saw the beads of perspiration standing out on his forehead. "You're making that up," he told her. "It didn't happen that way . . ."

Larcy said, "You had the weapon, Mr. Magnam. You were angry . . . afraid. Maybe you thought he'd come to . . . kill you."

He said fiercely, "She'd have used all of my money for that husband of hers. All of it. Anybody will tell you something like that's wrong, but she wouldn't listen to me. She never would listen to me."

His eyes narrowed, there was a wild, angry look on his thin, pain scarred face. He said, "He was going to kill me. They'd planned it . . . together, him and Bena."

He smiled grimly at Larcy. "I told you, didn't I, that anybody could get away with murder, that all they had to do was to find somebody with a motive and tie it on to them."

Larcy said quietly, "as you intend to . . . tie it on to Mrs. Pierce?" She turned away from him, went over to the medicine drawer, unlocked it, pretended to fill the syringe of the needle.

She turned and walked over to the bed, holding the needle carefully in one hand. She said, softly, softly, "You're in pain, Mr. Magnam, this will take away the pain."

He leaned back against the pillow, "Get that needle away from me!" he screamed at her. "You're not going to . . . kill me!"

Larcy wasn't prepared for the quickness of his move, the way he suddenly leaned to one side, coming up with the scissors held threateningly in his hand, lunging towards her.

The scream clawed its way out of her throat, went on and on. Larcy felt no more than the prick of the scissors as the point grazed her shoulder.

And then Pete was there, taking the scissors from David Magnam's suddenly limp hand, handing them to the detective, putting both arms, warm and comfortingly around Larcy.

Bena Pierce stood in the doorway. "What will happen to him?" she asked, shaking her head sadly.

"He'll be removed to a hospital," he said, "put under guard."

Bena said slowly, heavily. "It was wrong. Johnson had made his own way in the navy. The . . . talk probably wouldn't have mattered. I should never have let it . . . matter." She sighed, "You can't go back, can you, lieutenant? You can't . . . undo."

Pete put one arm around Larcy's waist. He looked over at the detective, said, "Can I take Larcy downstairs?"

When he nodded, Larcy turned to look at him, but what she said was for Bena Pierce. "I won't go too far, lieutenant. I have to . . . stay with him . . . Mr. Magnam until . . . they come for him."

Pete's arm tightened around her waist. Lyn had disappeared, as had Sybil. Larcy heard the detective's quiet, smooth voice say curtly, "Don't think you're out of it, Mrs. Pierce. You and your maid will be charged with being accessories after the fact. You had no right removing the body."

The sunlight poured in from the hall window as Larcy and Pete walked slowly down the stairs. Sand Lyn had tracked in sparkled on the hall floor, the picture of Johnson Pierce stared mockingly down from its place above the mantel in the living room.

Pete walked Larcy out the front hall, down the three steps to stand on the slight rise that led down to the lake.

Larcy said, a catch in her voice, "Will it . . . be too awful for her?"

Pete said, "No, I don't think so." And then, sternly, "The law has to be impartial, Larcy. She can't just

253

. . . get away with something because you happen to . . . feel sorry for her. No one can."

"I know," Larcy said. "I know."

Pete turned her slowly around so that she was facing him. His face bent towards her and then he was kissing her. The waves, as if newly released, pushed and prodded at the shore, laughter sounded from somewhere along the beach, an oar boat moved sluggishly down water towards port.

Pete's kiss went on and on, and sparks shot through Larcy. She said, sounding happy and bewildered at one and the same time, "Oh, my, fireworks!"

"Fireworks?" Pete lifted his head to stare down at her. "You're crazy, this isn't the Fourth of July."

Larcy blinked, said, a tremble in her voice, "That's what you think." And she lifted her lips to be kissed again.

LOOK FOR OUR MAGNUM CLASSICS

MACBETH by William Shakespeare
MASTER OF BALLANTRAE by Robert L. Stevenson
MASTER OF THE WORLD by Jules Verne
NORTHANGER ABBEY by Jane Austen
O. HENRY'S SHORT STORIES by O. Henry
PERSUASION by Jane Austen
PICTURE OF DORIAN GRAY by Oscar Wilde
POE'S TALES OF MYSTERY & TERROR
  by Edgar Allan Poe
PRISONER OF ZENDA by Anthony Hope
RED BADGE OF COURAGE by Stephen Crane
SILAS MARNER by George Elliot
STRANGE CASE OF DR. JEKYLL & MR. HYDE &
  OTHER STORIES by Robert L. Stevenson
TIME MACHINE by H. G. Wells
TOM SAWYER by Samuel L. Clemens
TOM SAWYER ABROAD & TOM SAWYER
  DETECTIVE by Samuel L. Clemens
TREASURE ISLAND by Robert Louis Stevenson
TURN OF THE SCREW & DAISY MILLER
  by Henry James
UP FROM SLAVERY by Booker T. Washington
VICAR OF WAKEFIELD by Oliver Goldsmith
WAR OF THE WORLDS by H. G. Wells
WHITE FANG by Jack London
WIND IN THE WILLOWS by Kenneth Grahame
WONDER BOOK by Nathaniel Hawthorne
WONDERFUL WIZARD OF OZ by L. Frank Baum